A Mountain of Gold

ORIGINAL STORY
BY
JAMES WADE HICKS

COAUTHORED BY
IAN F. WESLEY

CAMPIAN BELLSTONE PUBLISHERS
WWW.BELLSTONEBOOKS.COM

JAMES WADE HICKS

Dedicated to
my amazing wife, Sarah Patricia Hicks
&
Ian F. Wesley and his wonderful son,
Spencer

IAN F. WESLEY

Dedicated to
my friend and publishing collaborator
Fay Campbell
&
my dazzling buddy who completely surprised me
with this most inspiring story,
Jimmy Hicks

"Were there a mountain made of gold,
doubled, it would not be enough
to satisfy a single man.
Know this and live accordingly."

—Buddha

AMountainOfGold.com

Original story by James Wade Hicks
Coauthored by Ian F. Wesley
Edited by Fay Campbell
Cover art and interior illustrations by Steve Daniels

ISBN 978-1-940670-02-7

Campian Bellstone Publishers
www.BellstoneBooks.com

A MOUNTAIN OF GOLD
1. Historical Fiction   2. Youth Fiction
3. American History   4. Survival Stories

CONTENTS

PROLOGUE

My wife and I moved to the mountains of North Georgia in 2005. One day, I was taking a short hike on Brasstown Bald Mountain, which is the highest elevation in all of Georgia, and not far from my home. I was not on the paved road that goes to the top, but following a small creek just off the road, when I happened upon a furskin pouch.

At first I thought it was a dead rabbit or some sort of animal. I don't know why, but I moved it a bit with my walking stick. I then saw what looked like drawstrings. Most of the fur was worn off. I reached down and picked it up and felt something solid inside it. I untied and opened it, and found inside an antique box about ten inches long. It was lightly snowing that day, so I closed the pouch and walked up to the observation tower that is at the top of the mountain.

I went into the men's rest room where I took the box from the pouch. The corroded hinges broke when I pulled on the lid, and the outside of the box had some rot. The inside of the box was lined in a different material, perhaps bone or inlaid ivory, and in good condition. It contained about eighty small sheets of paper, six inches wide and nine inches long. Both sides of each sheet were covered in very small writing, mostly in faint pencil. I determined I would need my reading glasses and better light to see them clearly, so I returned them the box and took it and the pouch back home with me.

When I got home, I put my find on the dining room table and very carefully separated the sheets. The papers were brittle and slightly discolored, but still intact. Some of the writing was almost too faint to read. But I did read it, and it turned out to be part of a journal by a young man who lived in a mountain.

Yes, lived *in* a mountain.

I copied it word for word on my computer as best I could. My friend, editor/publisher Ian Wesley, had experience reading handwritten documents from the 1800s, and with his help I was able to read the more difficult sections. It was well written and the penmanship was very artful and consistent.

I don't know if this journal is fiction or an honest account of a boy's passage into adulthood, but I think it is a tale worth sharing. I divided it into chapters where divisions seemed appropriate and titled the book *A Mountain of Gold*.

Transcribing this very old journal made me interested in the local history it describes, namely the Georgia Land Lotteries and the tragic Trail of Tears. At the end of this book Mr. Wesley and I created a list of areas of study relevant to this fascinating diary, which learners of all ages might find useful.

I expect this story will be of particular interest to conservationists, naturalists, and history buffs, but it contains something for everyone, and readers of all ages should love it. It's my hope that this book provides fertile soil for discussion among its readers.

Let us now begin the journal of James Hill.

In the chapters of the journal are antiquated and obscure terms, flagged with asterisks (*), to indicate their inclusion in the Glossary in the back of the book.

A Mountain of Gold

Chapter 1
EARLY YEARS

I am 15 years old now, and I decided to write the story of my life growing up in the mountains of North Georgia. Father told me that we won the land in the Georgia Gold Land Lottery in 1832, and we had papers to prove it.

My father and my mother built a small cabin of logs by the creek. The logs were notched at the corners, and Father filled all of the cracks with little pieces of wood wedged in tightly so that no water would leak in. The roof was also made of logs, which were flat on the sides and fitted tightly against each other. The floor was dirt, which was pounded and packed down to make it smooth.

The front of the cabin faced south. There were two small, open windows, one on either side of the door. The west and north walls each had one small window. There was a stone fireplace on the east wall. In all, there were four windows, three feet square, with wooden shutters which could be shut fast* from the inside in case of storm or beast.

The shutters were made from planks held together with wooden pegs. These were hinged on the inside with leather straps at the top, and there were latches in each corner. When opened, the shutters were held by ropes from the ceiling. We opened them in the warm months, and we closed them in the winter.

By stepping it off, we reckoned the cabin was about 16 feet by 16 feet. There were no roads in or out. There were many big trees, and no one else— just the three of us.

Father and Mother brought all of his wood working tools and her books with them when they came to Georgia. They brought some of their clothes with them from England. Those were made of cloth. But the clothes we made in Georgia, as well as our shoes and boots, were made from animal hides.

Father made two beds—one for himself and mother to sleep in, and one for me. The beds had

wood frames with leathern* straps across the width of the bed, and longer straps woven the length of the frame. He stitched rabbit pelts to the straps, which made the beds quite comfortable. Father also made a table and three chairs.

My father named me James Hill, and I was born in 1834. My father's name was Mark Hill. My name came from the Holy Bible, so did my mother's and father's—James, Sarah and Mark. Sarah was the great mother of God's people. Mark and James were disciples of God's son on this earth, Jesus.

My father was thirty years old when I was born. Father was a big man with long, black hair and a long beard. He had a look of joy in his eyes, and the joy spread across his countenance* when he smiled.

Father told me that he was born in England and came here when he was twenty-eight years old. He told me that Mother and he came here on a big ship to the Port of Charleston, and by the next year they were in Georgia. I didn't know what a big ship looked like, so he drew a likeness of it on paper. Father was a cunning* artist, and the ship he drew appeared to stand on the page.

Father said that the ship could hold a multitude* of people and that it had vast,* hempen* sails that gathered the winds to move the vessel across the surface of the waters. He told me that a ship is like our cabin, yet manifold* in length and made with such craft* that no water can pass between its planks. The ship was pitched and painted for long voyages on the seas—waters so vast that no land can be seen for days, and men must pray by day to see stars by night or the ship may run astray. Father told me that it took 32 days to get to America—a long time not to see any land.

Father taught me to draw, and I spent much time in my youth taking pencil or charcoal to whatever I could find. Father, like his father, August, was a furniture maker for the very wealthy people in England. Mother and Father came here almost three years before I was born. They never told me why they left England.

My mother's name was Sarah, and she was twenty-eight years when I was born. She had long brown hair, brown eyes, and a beautiful smile. Mother was also born in England and had gone to a good school. In fact, Mother was a school teacher before coming to America.

Mother was my school teacher, too, and she started teaching me reading and writing when I was four years old. At first, she would read to me and show me pictures in the books that she had brought from England. She had little cards with the alphabet and numbers written upon them, that she had used to teach children in England. Mother had all the books she had used in England, including the

Holy Bible and the almanac.

By the time I was twelve years old, Mother had taught me reading, writing, penmanship, arithmetic, geometry, history, and natural history.* She told me that I was her best student ever. Mother and I studied in the daylight when I was very young, and into the night by lamp when I got older.

When I was big enough, I helped Father with his work—felling trees, sawing, building, planting and tending the garden, fishing, trapping, and making woven and leathern wares. Father would laugh and say, "From Mother you learn reading and writing, and from me righting and wroughting."*

Father and I set up a small waterwheel over the creek. The wheel was what he called an undershot waterwheel. The flowing water turned the wheel. When the creek was swift, the wheel could perform the work of three men, and it powered the sawmill we built to rip logs and make boards.

Father taught me about pulleys and how to use his wood working tools and how to take care of them. He also showed me how to make snares and cages from sticks to catch rabbits and other small animals. We made fish traps out of small reeds and used stone weights to suspend them just below the surface of the water. Father had a long-handled ax and a big knife—*the* knife. The knife was a little over a foot long from butt to tip, and he kept it sharp—so very sharp—using a flat stone.

Father taught me how to smoke fish in the fire pit he made. First, he dug a shallow hole outside the cabin about two feet across and laid flat stones around the hole. Next, he stacked up rocks around the perimeter of the flat stones, making a wall of rocks about two feet high all around. He made a wooden cover to place on the top. Finally, Father lit a slow fire and, when it was hot enough, added just enough water to nearly extinguish the fire. He then put the fish around the fire pit on the flat rocks and covered the structure to contain the abundance of smoke. The heat and smoke slowly cooked the fish very well and it was delicious!

When Mother cooked a turkey that way, it would be beautifully golden, and so tender that the meat fell off of the bones. It was so good with potatoes and carrots.

We had a nice garden that had potatoes, fine beans, corn, greens, and some other good things to eat. We also picked blueberries, blackberries, gooseberries, Chinese berries, mullberries, June berries and elderberries. Chestnuts were also in abundance on our land.

Father made two bows—one for him and one for me—for hunting, with many arrows. The bows were hewn,* carved, and polished pine and artfully made. Father was a fine craftsman.

Father also made slings out of deer hide. A hide pouch was tied in-between two straps. One of the straps ended in a loop that would be drawn fast* around the wrist. A river stone was placed in the pouch. Then, with one strap around the wrist and the end of the other strap held in the hand, the slinger* swings the sling around with great speed, then lets loose the end strap. The stone flies faster than can be thrown and can fell or kill most animals. There is a story in the Holy Bible about how the young David slew the giant, Goliath, with the same sort of sling, by which he became a hero and contender for kingship.

When I was about seven, Father taught me how to use a sling. He was expert, and I wanted to match his skill. Swinging straight and letting go at just the right time are the keys. Once, the stone hit me in the back of my leg! It took a couple of years, but I became really keen* at hitting whatever I sighted.

When I was twelve years old, I asked Father how I got here. Father told me then that when a man and a woman get married and live together, then he paused a long time and said, "Son, it takes a man and a woman to make a child, and we wanted to have a child, and *you* are that child. *God* gave you to us."

I said, "I think I understand, Father," but I really did not.

A few days later, Father and I spied two deer. The buck was trying to get on the back of the doe. I looked at Father and he looked at me. We were very still and watched.

In a little while the buck got down and started eating again. I asked Father why they did that. He said they were mating, and that in several months the doe would have her fawn, which would be either another doe or a buck. Then I understood. I didn't ask any more questions about from whence I came.

Chapter Two
OUR NEW HOME

One day, Father and I were checking our animal traps when Father saw a rabbit disappear down a hole. Father looked into the hole, which was just big enough for one person to crawl into. Father put his feet in first, then lowered himself down to his shoulders and told me to stay where I was. He dropped to his knees and said he could see only a little way, but enough to see that the hole expanded as a tunnel. He stood up and crawled out.

Father always carried his pack, in which he carried several needful items—a sack for collecting things, some twine, a tinderbox* for lighting fires, among other things. Father gathered up some sticks and handed them to me. Then he reached into his pack and took out the tinderbox and a handful of small pieces of dried wood—plane shavings and whittling chips—for kindling. He made a clearing on the ground where we built a small fire, then I helped him fashion a torch. When the torch was lit, he handed it to me. Father then got back in the hole and I handed the torch to him. He crouched down and crawled a short distance, then returned to tell me we had found a cave of some size. He told me once more to stay put while he investigated a bit further.

When he reappeared, he told me to get some more sticks together and light another torch, as the first was about to burn out. I did so, and as I handed it to Father, he said with a smile, "Come on in with me!"

I was filled with excitement as I crawled into the hole behind Father. The tunnel was not too long, and led over a small mound of rocks. Then the cave expanded to where we could stand up. The ceiling was about ten feet tall. The cave widened out to about twenty feet and was perhaps thirty feet in length.

We looked about and I wondered where the rabbit had gone. That moment I saw something move at the far end of the cave. It was the rabbit, which ran through another hole that was just big enough for its body.

Father declared as he surveyed the cavern, "This could make our new home. It's much bigger than our cabin, and it would be a lot warmer in the winter and cooler in the summer. It's very safe, too. A person could walk right by the entrance and never see it." (Father was right about missing the entrance. I have done it time after time, and I live here!)

Father told me, "No matter what, do not ever tell a living soul where this cave is."

I wondered how could I tell anyone. I had never seen anyone but Father and Mother. There was no one to tell!

Father and I walked back to tell Mother about our new home. When Father told her about it, she exclaimed, "Live in a cave?"

Father said, "Just wait until you see it. It is three times the size of our cabin. I can build a fire pit to keep us warm and cook our food. James can have his own area to sleep in, and we can have our own area. We can have larger places for eating, reading, working, and we will be more comfortable summers and winters."

Mother reluctantly admitted it all sounded promising and asked to go see it.

"Not yet," said Father. "Let James and me make a fire pit first, so that you can see just how nice your new home will be."

Mother asked if we were hungry. We had been so excited about the cave, that we hadn't noticed the rabbit stew on the pit. It smelled wonderful and made us realize how hungry we were.

As we ate our stew, Father said the first thing we must do is bore a hole in the top of the cave to make a chimney, then use some of the rocks from the tunnel to build the fire pit beneath the chimney hole.

Once back at the cave, Father cut the hole from the inside so that any rocks and dirt that fell could be used in making the fire pit. It took a long time to cut the hole, because the ceiling of the cave was hard clay, and he used only a pointed stick.

Father bored a hole about six inches across,

about three feet into the ceiling. Then he placed me on his shoulders to dig higher. My arms and shoulders ached, but when the chimney was about five feet into the ceiling, the evening sun broke through. We laughed and cheered.

We were very weary from boring upward through five feet of clay, but having finished the hard part, we now had new energy from our excitement. We quickly cleared the spot for the fire pit and made a low, half-circle wall of rocks and stones for the pit and then laid up the rest to make a chimney. Now the smoke would be directed up and not go into the rest of our new home.

We lit kindling in the pit—our first fire in our new home—and then stacked in many sticks and a log. We stood back and looked around the cave in the firelight, and commended each other on our day's accomplishment. Our timing was perfect. It was just getting dark, but we had enough time to get Mother.

When she first saw the cave, she was impressed with its size as well as the warm, welcoming glow of the fire.

The next day we moved all of our things to our new home. That evening we had dinner, then all sat by the fireplace. It was cold outside, but was warm in the cave.

In high winds, strong rains, and very cold days, our cabin would creak and sometimes whistle. Leaks and drafts would often trouble us. But our new home offered us peace and silence and ample space to keep firewood dry and ready.

Father started to read aloud from the Holy Bible. He read from the book of James. It is a short book. Father said that this was the right and the true way to live our lives.

Chapter 3
A POT OF GOLD

Mother was the prettiest woman I'd ever seen, but then, I had never seen any other women. Her face was smooth and soft.

I recall Mother singing a song to me when I was young about a rainbow and a pot of gold. It was a happy little song.

> Rainbow, rainbow,
> Far dost thou measure.
> Lucky shall he be
> That findeth under thee
> Thy pot of golden treasure.

Mother said that there was a pot of gold at the end of the rainbow, and maybe we could find it one day. I asked Mother about this pot of gold, and she told me that a pot of gold was worth a tremendous amount of money, and that money could be traded to buy things like food and tools and horses. I asked Mother, "Why would anyone buy food? Why not just make a garden, fish and set out some traps?"

Mother laughed, then shrugged and said, "Well, some people are just lazy, I guess," then she added, "And few are as blessed as we."

One day, just after it had stopped raining, there it was—a beautiful rainbow in the sky! I thought of mother's song and the pot of gold, so right away I ran as fast as I could toward the end of the rainbow. I knew rainbows remained only briefly, so I hurried to find that pot of gold! I ran and I ran, and I ran some more—up hill and down hill, and I even jumped an unfamiliar stream. Yet I never seemed to get close to the rainbow. It always seemed to be just one or two hills away. I became too tired to run, and saw as I reached the top of a high hill, that the rainbow had vanished.

In discouragement I turned around to head back home, but, where was home? I had run beyond anywhere I had been before. The landscape was not familiar. At the start of my run I didn't think whether I was running east, west, north, or south.

Surrounded by trees and with no landmarks, I was surely lost!

I stood very still and shut my eyes, as Father taught me to do, and I listened hard. I soon heard my mother's distant voice calling, "James, James, where are you?" I could just barely hear her.

I called back to her, "Here I am, Mother!" I started to run down the hill, but then I stopped. There was a bear about fifty feet in front of me! There was a fallen tree limb to my side with a lot of leaves on it, so I picked up the branch and I started running toward the bear, hollering as loud as I could. The bear looked puzzled and startled, and it ran the other way.

Father told me that if I ever saw a bear when I was alone, to either stand very still or pick up something to make me appear larger, and make a lot of noise. And that is what I did.

As I was half-way up the next hill, I shut my eyes and listened again for Mother's voice. I listened long, but didn't hear it. Instead, I heard something coming toward me. When I open my eyes, there she was right in front of me! She held me tight and told me that she, too had seen the bear and had watched as I frightened it away. She was trembling a bit, but I told her that I was all right, and that I would take her home. She laughed and said, "All right, my little man." She hugged me again with a beaming smile that made me forget all my disappointment at not finding a pot of gold. We walked home together, so happy to have each other.

"Which way did I run, Mother?" I asked.

"West, I think. What made you run away?"

"I wanted to find the pot of gold," I said.

Mother laughed, "You dear! When the time is right in your life, gold will surely find you. You don't have to chase it."

Not long after my rainbow-chasing lesson, Mother came down with a bad cough. It became worse, and she was not well enough to rise from her bed. On the third day, when Father and I came home from the garden, she was shivering, though she had wrapped herself up in two fur covers, and was sweating. Father told me to build a fire and get some water.

When I turned to obey my father, I looked at

my mother. She was looking back at me. She shut her eyes and whispered, "James, I love you."

I answered, "I love you too, Mother."

I quickly stoked the fire as Father remained at her bedside. I went outside to fetch water from the creek, about a minute's walk from the opening of the cave. When I returned with a full bucket, I saw my father on his knees, holding Mother, and he was crying. I had never seen Father cry before. So I came to his side and asked with fear, "Father, why are you crying?"

He looked up and said, "Son, your mother has gone to live with Jesus in heaven."

"Father," I said, "She is right here."

He said, "What you see is just her body. Her soul has gone to be with Jesus, where she will live very happily and forever."

I said, "Oh, that is good," but I only felt confusion. I had seen many dead animals before, of course, but never a dead person. My dear mother's eyes had that same emptiness I'd seen on other creatures, and I wondered how it was that Father was sure she was in heaven, but he never said the this about an animal. The emptiness seemed the same, why would the fates be different?

That evening I helped Father build a box out of oak planks that he had sawed for the new dining table. I handed him the dowels as he put the box together. We lined the inside with furs and made a pillow for Mother's head, and then we laid Mother in the box and closed the lid.

Father stayed up that night digging the grave. The next morning we buried Mother. Father said a prayer. I couldn't say anything. I just stood by. I can't describe the feelings I had. The thought of never seeing my mother again was unbearable. I loved her so much. She taught me things that my father just didn't know.

Chapter 4
FATHER AND I

*A*fter we buried Mother, we went back inside. Father opened the Holy Bible and read the opening verses of St. John chapter 14:

> Let not your heart be troubled: ye believe in God, believe also in me. In my Father's house are many mansions: if it were not so, I would have told you. I go to prepare a place for you. And if I go and prepare a place for you, I will come again, and receive you unto myself; that where I am, there ye may be also.

That promise comforted me for a time, but soon I began crying again. My throat burned as fire. I drank some water I had fetched for my mother, and said aloud, "Why!" In my mind I was asking why God would let this happen. God must have known how much I needed Mother and loved her. I kept reminding myself that she was with Jesus in heaven, and that she was happy. The thought did make me feel better, but I knew that I was going to miss Mother every day, though she would always be with me in spirit.

For the next year it was Father and me. We hunted, fished, trapped, and skinned the animals. We grew our garden and dried most of the fruits and vegetables when we harvested them.

At night I read and studied Mother's school books and practiced my penmanship. I had read all of our books at least twice, and I was hungry to learn more.

Before winter came, Father made a journey to Blairsville to sell skins, pelts, leathern and other wares, so he could purchase rope, twine, and tools. I remained behind to tend to our garden.

He returned a week later and presented me with a stack of fresh drawing paper and two new books. The first was a large, leather-bound tale of adventure and exploration of the seas by Captain Thomas Forrest, *A Voyage to New Guinea*. Its full title was:

A Voyage to New Guinea
and the Moluccas, from Balambangan,
including an Account of Magindano,
Sooloo, and Other Islands

The book was illustrated with thirty copperplate prints. This book gave me new visions of ships to behold, but none as fine, in my esteem, as the drawing of a ship my father made.

The second book was smaller, also bound in leather, and had no printed title. It contained famous political tracts and letters by notable Virginians, such as George Wythe, Thomas Jefferson, George Mason, and George Washington. I learned Wythe, who became a mentor to many great Americans, was, like I, educated mostly by his mother.

I realized my father bought these books so I might have new things to contemplate after the loss of my mother, and to honor her by continuing to learn. Father spent more acquiring our new paper and books than he did on our other supplies, but he was proud and happy to give me them. With Mother gone, he took a greater interest in reading. I could see he missed her sorely, as did I.

We took delight in discussing all of the books in the cave together. As we read in the large book about the naval encounters with the island people of the East, Father couldn't help feeling sad for what might lay ahead for them in trading with the West, drawing from the fates of America's first peoples. He explained to me that many Americans thought themselves superior to the native peoples, and any people with darker skin. He explained it, but it didn't make sense to me. I wondered how people who believe that all humans are made in the image of God could believe that some humans are superior to others.

My book by Virginians made us solemnly question how our fellow English Americans treated the natives of this land and the Negroes still in slavery these 65 years since independence was won. Thomas Jefferson wrote:

> I tremble for my country when I reflect that God is just; that his justice cannot sleep forever.

Father also showed me different techniques in his art work during this time. He conveyed perspective and shadows skillfully. He said my work was as fine as his, but maybe that was only his opinion, brightened by his love for me, his only companion.

Chapter 5
CIVILIZATION

The next year, when I was just turning 15 years old, Father made another trip to Blairsville, and this time he took me with him. He said I was due for a taste of civilization. I had never been to a town since I could remember. He had a tremendous surplus of seed and would sell it and 35 pelts from trapping. Now that I was tall and strong I could help carry the load.

As we traveled, I was full of new questions, including why some people live in towns, and why towns are built where they are. He answered these questions, and told me again about Blairsville, but this time he told me how the land was taken from Indians, and he told me what he knew about the Trail of Tears. It sounded to me like a horrible injustice, and from what I have read in my book of Virginians, I found it hard to believe Father understood it properly. I wanted to learn more about it.

We traveled westward. Father showed me how to locate the western direction by the sunset and also by the stars. He had taught me such things many years earlier, but this was my first time to use this knowledge to travel beyond where I could see. I had never been more than one or two hills beyond the boundary of our own land since I could walk.

We walked quickly. Father said it was a two-day trip for the swift of foot. At every mountain ridge Father would point where the path before us would lie, and he was careful to avoid settlements. He said prospectors lived through here and were hostile to all strangers. Prospectors were determined to find gold no matter what they had to do to get it.

We followed streams and the treelines of meadows. At night we stopped at a lake to camp. Since our packs were so large, we brought little provision for ourselves. Aside from the pelts and seeds, we had only Father's knife, a dozen empty sacks and pouches, a copper pan and cup, the tinderbox, twine, and a hat and a fresh shirt for Father. I brought but one luxury for myself, though I counted it needful. I brought a pencil and two leaves of paper, so I could write about all the new things I saw.

Father said he would take me to a haberdasher* for a coat and hat, so I wouldn't be mistaken for a savage.

Father built a fish snare where the river met the lake. I didn't believe that was what he was building, because at home our fish snares were made with fine reeds. He made this one much larger, and of the sturdiest reeds, and to my amazement caught the biggest fish I had ever seen! High in the mountains where we lived, most fish were shiners, barely as long as a man's finger. This fish, a lake trout, was as long as my forearm. He said it was ten pounds, and that trout in big lakes are even larger. Half of that single fish was supper for the both of us that evening, and the other half Father threw into the lake for other fish to eat. We didn't think again of food until high noon on the morrow.

By then, we had found the road, and as we walked it, we saw people ahead of us. I was most enthused, but Father bade* me stay our pace and not hail* them. He said other travelers are accustomed to seeing others near towns and cities, and that it was only exciting for me. He said many people travel just to have time away from the clamour and pressure of civilization.

The road had ruts, which Father explained were from wagon wheels and so many people walking there. Now and then, we'd see droppings from horses, donkeys and other draught animals. I noticed there were no woods nearby. The lands around the road were farms, and in the fields, at great distance, I could see people, as many as twenty, working in them. I had never seen so many people before at once glance.

What wasn't farmland was a haunting sight. Where forests and woods once stood, there was now only barren hills spangled* with stumps. Thousands upon thousands of trees had been felled, and nothing stood in their place. I knew what effort was required to fell a single oak or walnut, and to see countless stumps brought me fear.

In the distance, in the middle of the field, was a heap of something, maybe livestock, and above it were about 30 vultures circling, joining others atop the heap. I asked Father what unfortunate creatures they might be, and he said he wouldn't know.

The road widened, and ahead I saw a horse cart approaching. On the cart was a man with a gray and black beard wearing a fur hat and black coat. As we neared each other, I could tell that his cart was empty, except for a man with dark brown skin. The driver had unloaded his wares in Blairsville, perhaps. Following him was a foal, wearing a halter which was tied to the cart. The man looked at the two of us, wearing our very large packs, then halted his horse.

"Good day, sirs," he called to us.

Father kept walking, but tipped his hat to the man.

"Wurd you good men be in want of a horse?" asked he with a strange accent.

"No, thank you," answered Father. "I have no use for a horse."

As we passed the man, I admired his animals and the construction of the wheels of his cart. They were both iron and hardwood. I wondered what large load the man may have hauled to need a horse and cart to move it.

Then, I looked up for the very first time at a man with dark skin. He looked indifferent to us and tired. His attire was of simple hemp cloth. I knew this was a Negro man, and that he had no say in going on this errand. He was a man's property. This mystified me. Father would not even own a horse. I smiled and waved at the Negro man, but he looked at me the way Father did the day I brought a wounded mountain lion cub into our cabin. I would remember both his expression and Father's for the rest of my life.

After Father bade* the driver good day and the cart was well behind us, I asked Father about the man.

"He was German," Father replied. "Many Germans live in these parts and to the north." Father also speculated that the cart man had transported milled goods.

I asked about the brown man. Father confirmed he was surely a slave. I asked Father how our Christian nation could have slaves, when the Holy Bible tells that God delivered men from slavery, and did so by smiting* their masters.

Father sighed and said, "Jesus told men to repay evil with good. It is God who repays evil. His reward will come, and I hope we are spared from seeing it." He looked at my face and could tell I wanted more of an answer. "If your mother and I had raised you around slaves, and taught you it was right, you would probably think it's the proper order of things."

"Does every white family have brown servants?" I asked.

Father shook his head, tiring of my many questions, "No, James. Most white people do not have slaves."

Soon, the road became level and flat. I also asked Father how this was done.

"Corduroy,"* he said, "or planks. It's split logs covered with sand, so the way is solid and smooth and no wagons suffer damage near the town.

The town itself was a sight! There were painted signs on the road, between and sometimes on the buildings. The town was even larger than I had imagined. There must have been thirty buildings in one place, and most of them were two storeys* high! There were people, horses, and wagons in the thoroughfare,* and three or four other streets adjoined the main. The side streets were entirely mud and manure—not a spot of grass to walk upon! Any soul who treads those ways would return home soiled to the knees. One might think to grow potatoes in their laundry!

I asked Father which was the haberdashery,* and he only laughed in reply. He seemed to know the town, and walked us directly to a green-painted building in the center of town. Across from it, to my surprise, was a charred shell of a building.

"Father!" I exclaimed. "What happened there?"

"Town Hall must have burned down," he said, "and not long ago. It was the largest building in the town. I wonder how it happened."

Quickly, I realized the temper of the townfolk was sour. A woman not much older than I hurried past us carrying linens, and her face was in tears. I wanted so much to greet her, but she was in peril.

"Give me your pack, James," said Father, "I'll be about an hour. Don't go far." He carried both our packs into the green building, a store. I stood before its porch, watching the desperate lady knock at the door of a house beside the burnt building.

The lady entered the house, and moments later the door opened again. Two large men carried what appeared to be a dead person, covered in the linens, on a long plank. When I understood the grief of the woman, I too wept as I remembered helping Father carry Mother to her grave.

I entered the store to tell Father what I had seen, but was so suddenly and thoroughly taken aback by the place that I couldn't speak. The interior was a large room, in which two cabins could have fit, and in stacks and on shelves were all manner of goods and artifices,* and in great numbers!

In one bundle were ten shovels. Four hand axes lay on a small table, and against the wall were three stacks of fine wooden chairs, five high! Neatly folded were blankets, linens, pillows, quilts—some plain, some embroidered, some dyed, some in patterned weaves, and in American, European, and Cherokee styles. There were cedar chests large enough to hide a person, trunks for travel, baskets, lanterns, pots, spades, hoes, bridles, stirrups, saddles, wares of brass, copper, tin, silver, and behind a great counter was a sign:

WE TRADE WELL
FOR YOUR GOLD

The counter had glass walls, and inside them were pistols, knives, powder horns, timepieces, and jeweled ornaments for ladies. Seated in a corner was a very large man with a styled mustache, and on his lap was a shotgun. It was my first time to see a firearm outside of a book. He was looking at me as well. I reckoned he was there to guard the property.

I heard Father's voice and followed it to the back of the great room, where he was in conversation with a rotund gentleman with very orange hair and an even more spectacular mustache. Behind them was a pair of bookshelves with glass doors that covered their contents. There must have been more than 200 books! The top shelf of the case on the left contained a number of Holy Bibles, maybe ten! On the shelf beneath them were psalters, hymnals, and a German Bible. On the next shelf were books by famous Americans—Governor William Bradford, Edward Taylor, Cotton Mather, Benjamin Franklin, and Charles Brockden Brown. There were almanacs, atlases, natural histories, books of law and history, and a book about medicine with the names Hippocrates, Galen, Razes, and da Vinci. There was a book about machines, which I so much wanted to see. There was also a book that had the longest title:

A Brief Historical, Statistical and
Descriptive Review of East Tennessee,
United States of America, Developing
Its Immense Agricultural, Mining, and
Manufacturing Advantages,
with Remarks to Emigrants.

At the bottom of the case were books in other languages—French, German, Spanish, Latin, and Greek. The other case was full of books for schooling children, reading for ladies, journals, and several small books wrapped in brown paper, which were a mystery.

"Your little Indian is fond of writing," came a deep voice behind me. It was the large man who had been talking to Father. His accent was different than Father's or the German driver's.

"Writing all he sees," Father said, and squeezed my shoulder with pride. I don't know how long they spoke while I wrote on my paper so many titles and authors of books.

I stood and faced the large man, who smiled at me. "Good day, sir," I said.

"Aye," he replied. "Fancy a book, lad?"

"Oh, many, sir. I want to read as many books as Mr. Jefferson."

"Well, come back often, then. We have a fine array, as great as any place in Charleston or Chattanooga." Then he nodded and walked through a door, above which was a sign that read "BLACKSMITH." Father followed him. I followed them.

The room was full of iron works. There were baskets and wooden boxes of iron nails, screws, chains, pokers, grates, ploughs, hinges, latches, candle stands, and on the wall was a fancy iron cross. It made me think of the cross Father scratched on the stone above Mother's grave.

"Oh, Father," I said, remembering. "In the house by the burnt building, I saw them carry out a dead person!"

"Oh?" asked Father.

"Yellow fever," said the storekeep. "It's bad this year, and early. It's why our stocks are so high. Folk are afraid to come out. That was Mrs. Strauss." Then he shouted into the great room, "Charley, add Hannah Strauss to the list!"

"Already did, Uncle," the gunman shouted back.

This was frightening to hear. I had read about yellow fever, and Father told me stories of it. "How many have died?" I couldn't help but ask.

"Thirty now, maybe thirty-two," the man answered solemnly. "We have a month, maybe two, before it's over. It's really bad. Y'know last year in Charleston half of the great Lutheran Church died of it. Half the congregation of more than six hundred!" Then he smiled again, adding, "Oh, and we still have two bottles left of quinine and of laudanum. They'll sure as George be gone by tomorrow."

"No, thank you," said Father.

I remained in the smithy* as Father resumed his negotiations with the proprietor. In the livestock section I saw a branding iron. A sign on the wall read "We Can Forge Your Mark." Another sign read "We Repair Cotton Gins." Beside the iron were bellows of different sizes on the wall, and beside them were curious curved bands. I studied them for a minute before realizing they were not fetters* for beasts, but for human wrists and ankles. There was also a wrought iron bar with three hinged fetters for two wrists and a neck. I tried to imagine how these things must be used—chains, manacles, brands—and my throat became tight and my heart faint.

I wanted to leave the store, so I went back outside. I stood on the porch again and saw a two-horse cart passing. On the cart were seven long, pine boxes. I remembered the box Father had made for Mother, and I grew sorrowful again, and couldn't look any longer.

I began to walk in the opposite direction on the thoroughfare and soon saw a building that I recognized as a church. It was painted white, its front windows were many colours, and on its roof was a spire reaching higher than anything else in the town. The front doors were open, so I approached.

For the first time I was about to set foot into a house of God. I remembered what God had told Moses when they first met:

> Put off thy shoes from off thy feet, for the place whereon thou standest is holy ground.

So I removed my boots and left them outside. With gentle steps I entered the vestibule. I had no notion what would be inside. I had seen a drawing of the inside of a cathedral before, but that was in a book, and a drawing doesn't show life. A drawing of a deer is much different than seeing a living deer. I thought perhaps the living presence of God would be visible inside God's house. I thought that in the church, God might be closer to me, and I would be closer to my Mother.

I walked into the middle of the hall with my eyes low, then raised my head. Tall, coloured windows surrounded me, and there were benches where nearly 100 people could sit. The ceiling was high, and behind a platform on a white wall was a great, black-stained cross. This startled me. I knew crosses were on the covers of Bibles and carried by priests and some pastors, but I didn't think God would put one in His house, the very device on which his son was killed! I stepped back with anxiety and looked down at the floor again. I didn't want to see a cross, but something from the living God.

"What the hell are you doing in here?" came a man's voice, loud and sharp.

I turned to see a man dressed in black standing in the vestibule.

"No Indians!" the man yelled.

I looked behind myself to see if an Indian was also in the church. I was alone in the sanctuary.

"Get your filth out of this sacred hall right now!" the man hollered. "You godless heathens brought this pestilence on us, and now you dare try to spoil this house of refuge!"

I realized he was shouting at me, and in fear I passed through the vestibule to leave. "I am not an Indian, sir," I said, holding back tears of fright.

The man, bald and wrinkled, stood very tall, taller than Father. He was the first old man I had ever seen. He looked sour and stern. "Half breed! Don't try to excuse yourself!" Then he smacked me in the head and pushed me out the door.

My deerskin boots were gone. I looked about and found them in the thoroughfare. As I collected them, I turned back to the church, wanting to explain myself to its guardian, and saw him coming out of its doors in my direction, carrying a broom, with an expression that said he intended me harm.

"I am White!" I screamed. "My name is James Hill and I am here with my father, Mark Hill!"

The old guard stopped. My English accent must have persuaded him more than my reddish hair, but his face turned even more drawn. "Maybe you are, but who but a *heathen* would enter the house of the Lord dressed and smelling like a filthy Indian!?"

"Reverend Calhoun!" shouted a woman's voice. As I walked away from the church carrying my boots, I saw the woman who had been crying. She was crying again. The old man's countenance softened, and he addressed the lady by name and greeted her with unexpected tenderness. I realized he was the pastor of the church.

As I returned to the store to find Father, I decided not to put my boots back on. The street was finer than any path I'd traveled back home, and my boots needed to air after traveling. As I reached the porch, Father came through the door with a full sack.

Father smiled at me, then saw my face, and his smile disappeared. "James?"

I was crying for the first time since Mother died.

"What is wrong, Son?"

I didn't know how to begin. My first thought was the crying woman. "I'm scared ... scared of yellow fever." It wasn't a lie; I was scared of yellow fever, but that wasn't why I was crying. I couldn't tell him about the hateful, monstrous man in black who hit me and shoved me and called me a heathen, just for wearing the clothes Father made for me. Those were the harshest words any person had ever spoken to me. I thought that a haberdashery should have been our first stop.

"Do you wish to leave now?"

I nodded to Father, sobbing.

"That's fine," he said. "Put your boots back on and we'll make the lookout by nightfall. I have fresh corn bread and some peaches. We'll have a joyful time."

As we walked out of the town, I worried that I had disappointed Father. He had promised me I would stay with him in an inn, have a hot bath in a tub, hear a piano, and taste beefsteak and chocolates.

I looked at my father. My eyes were level with his nose. He looked at me with anxiety. "Are you disappointed?" I asked him.

He laughed. "No, James. I was worried *you* were disappointed!" He put his arm around my shoulder.

Peaches and corn bread suited me fine.

"So, what did civilization cause you to think?" asked Father.

I thought about my short time in the town, and how people mistook me for a savage. I answered, "It made me think to write the story of my life. And that I'll begin when we get home."

Chapter 6
BEING MY OWN TEACHER

Now that Mother was not here anymore, I became keenly interested in continuing to learn on my own, especially about Nature and science. I now realize how much I love learning, because the universe is so large and so beautiful. No matter where I look, the infinite varieties of life are magnificent—the colours, the patterns, the textures, the fragrances of flowers, the design and movements of animals. Even the sounds of Nature filled me with wonder—the booming of thunder, the rustling of trees in the wind, the chortling of a brook, the humming of bees, the songs of birds, the shrieks of the hawks, the chanting crickets and frogs at night, the wails of wild dogs, and the roar of the bears.

Father didn't tell me until we were home, but

in the Blairsville store, he had bought for me a coat, a hat, a wedge of chocolate, and best of all, a book about Nature by the famed Alexander von Humboldt:

COSMOS:
A Survey of the General History
of the Universe

It was translated into English, of course. In it, Mr. von Humboldt related his travels in the sunniest latitudes of the globe, and had this to say of Ethiops and other dark-skinned peoples on page 107:

> Heat of sun in the tropical world, and dark colour of skin, seemed inseparable.

This I found to be revelatory. The reason brown people are brown is because they come from the sunniest lands! Had I been born to a people between the Tropics of Cancer and Capricorn, I would be brown, perchance as dark as my wedge of chocolate.

The Indian peoples are a middling colour, between what folk wrongly call white, and what they wrongly call black, and the Indians live most of their lives naked in the sun. Whites are Europeans, who

have lived many centuries covered from crown to toe. I can't in all my imaginings propose that wearing much clothing makes a people better than those who don't. Since our visit to Blairsville, I couldn't forget the unbecoming treatment I'd received simply because a White man thought I was an Indian, and the harsh iron implements at the smithy for slaves, some of whom aren't even half Brown. If I, a European, can live so well the life of an Indian, then a Red or Brown man can live as a White! And Jesus, being from a people who for centuries lived on the borders of deserts, must have been Red, himself.

My day among civilization didn't persuade me at all that Whites are better than Reds and Blacks. I am ashamed that I shouted to that horrible old man that I wasn't an Indian. I do live like an Indian, and I think myself better for it, and I boldly suppose that I love Jesus more than he does. I will take a beating before I ever again rely on my colour for lenience!

I told my father my thoughts about the colours of men, and Father said he was sure my thinking was right. I showed him that I had begun writing the story of my life. He helped me create a binding for it of rabbit skin.

He also encouraged me to make a journal and chronicle my findings in Nature, as many botanists and naturalists like von Humboldt were doing. We didn't have an encyclopaedia of flora and fauna, though I had seen them in the store. Father told me these were now quite popular. Men of science were earnestly compiling catalogues of natural history, with detailed drawings and descriptions of animals, plants, peoples and landscapes from every land. In addition to writing my own life story, I would draw and describe our Georgian wildlife, and perhaps one day it might be published.

Chapter 7
BIG BEAR

O h, how hard it is to write! But to whom but you, my precious paper, can I tell this?

On the last full moon, Father and I were out to pick some wild blueberries. Earlier that day I had found them, but I didn't have anything to put them in, so I went back to get Father to help me pick them. The sun was setting when we came to where the blueberries were—a small clearing in the woods thick with berry bushes all around.

Father was congratulating me for this find as I walked ahead of him, at which time I heard a noise. Suddenly, the biggest bear that I had ever seen was on top of Father! I was about twenty feet away, and it happened so fast that I could not think what to do or say. My father had already taken his knife in-hand before the bear appeared, and I hoped he

could protect himself.

I saw him slashing at the great bear, but in a moment, Father's arm fell limp. The bear seemed hurt and hobbled a short distance away into the trees. I ran to my father, only to see that the bear had bit right into Father's face. It was horrible! I shouted in the direction the bear had gone, with more rage than fear. I heard it move farther away.

I knelt beside Father, but I dared not look at his face. He lay there, not moving at all, and the pool of blood under him grew large. It was awful, so awful. I didn't know what to do.

I said, "Father, you were mauled by a bear. What should I do?" As I feared, he didn't answer, didn't move. I placed my hand on his chest, but felt no breath. I quickly glanced and saw the terrible truth—most of his face was gone.

I got sick and vomited. After I threw up I saw a trail of blood leading into the woods. I took the knife from beside Father's lifeless hand. It was sticky with blood. I wanted to kill that bear or die trying.

I took not thirty steps before I found it. I was so confused. The bear did not move. She just lay there. "God, what is happening?" I asked in tearful disbelief.

I heard something approaching, something smaller. I turned, holding the knife before me. A young bear cub emerged from the bushes and slowly moved over to the bear, sniffing as it neared. The cub was so very small.

As I stood there, I thought, "What I am going to do?" It was getting late. The daylight was vanishing, and I could not just leave Father there. It was a cool night, but not cold, so I just sat there all night, watching over him.

The bear cub lay beside his slain mother, while I, in the dark of night and through bitter tears, covered Father's head with a canvas satchel from his pack.

It was not easy to sit near my poor father's body. I would often walk back into the woods where the she-bear lay, and beside her the hapless cub. I looked at the cub and wondered what would become of him, and then wondered more so, what would happen to me.

The night was ever so long. Many times I thought to dig a grave there in the woods, but the clay under the soil was like rock, and I had no tools for digging. It was a most terrible night for me—the last night of my childhood.

At the first light I decided to carry Father to a ravine not far from where we were. I would bury him there.

My God! It was awful—I could not get him up, and his body was beginning to stiffen. I could not believe that this had happened. I finally got Father's body to my shoulder and began to walk. The first twenty feet were down hill, and the rest of the journey was up hill, all the way to the ravine. When I got Father there, I lay him down as gently as I could.

How? How could this be? How could my precious, wonderful father now be this wretched carcass? I was shaking. My knees were weak and I thought that I was going to vomit again. I became very sick in my belly and fell down beside Father and started to cry again. I knew that it would be the last time that I would ever be with him in this world, so I told him that I dearly loved him and that I was really scared.

I then looked around to see how I was going to cover him. There were a multitude of small rocks, so I took some and laid them all around him, then put some sticks on top and covered the sticks with more rocks. It took me a long time to finish.

I said farewell to Father, too exhausted to cry, and left the ravine.

On the way home, I remembered the bear and the bear cub and realized Father's pack was still at the blueberry patch, so I turned back to retrieve it. It lay three feet from a forbidding, brown-stained patch of moss; the sunlit site was buzzing with flies.

I heard a cry from the woods and knew it was the cub. I walked toward the black heap of bear, where the confused, hungry cub still sat. As I approached, the cub moved away. I could see that the mother bear was dead, and I wanted to kick the corpse in my anguish. I stood there shaking in my anger, hunger, tiredness, and sorrow.

"It's so big. Why is it dead?" I asked, confused. I couldn't make myself remember what I had seen last evening, so I couldn't figure out what had killed the bear so far from my father. I stared until a memory formed in my mind. I recalled seeing something shine just for a split second. Then it came to me—it was father's knife. He must have mortally wounded the bear during their brief, deadly struggle.

I had seen Father skin a deer before, and wondered if Father's last act had been to open the bear's belly. I had to know for myself that the bear was truly dead, and if it was, exactly how my father did it.

A heavy, putrid, sickening stench, unlike anything I'd experienced before, filled the air and made my empty stomach convulse. I walked around the massive corpse, trying not to breathe too deeply, as I inspected it with my hands. There was indeed a long gash in the bear's belly, and out of it was spilt* some of her intestines. Another gash, much smaller, was at the bear's neck. I then knew the blood that was all over Father's knife was the bear's blood.

I really needed to wash. The stench of the bear's rotting innards and the horror of the night before clung to me. So I walked to the creek, which was about an hundred* feet away, and washed my arms and face in the chilling water. My leathern pants, my moccasins, Father's knife—all were covered with blood. I took them off and washed them in the creek. I stood there, naked and shivering. I wrung out my clothes, but had to put them on wet, which made me feel even colder. The discomfort was small compared to having watched my father die.

I started to walk home. Sunset began. I was hungry, but I didn't want to eat. I just wanted to get warm again, then sleep. In the morning I would use Father's knife to skin the bear.

As I crawled down into the cave, I thought again of the cub. I was about sixteen and he was just a cub without a mother to take care of him. What could I do? I brushed the thought from my mind. I was so tired, wet, and cold.

I knew that I had to light the pit, but where was the flint? It was dark in the cave—completely dark. I felt my way to where we kept the tinderbox and put my hands on it. From there I also found the bundle of straw for starting new fires. I flicked and flicked the flint. It sparked each time, and finally the straw caught fire. I blew on the embers gently and was glad to see the flame! I added some more sticks. Night had fallen, and the air was getting cooler, so the warmth from the fire pit felt especially good.

I took off all my wet clothes and set them by the fire, then placed larger sticks and a log into the pit. I crawled into my bed and covered up with the skins, which felt good against my bare skin.

As I lay there, thoughts of my father came rushing in.

Why?

Why, why, why why?

I reflected that I was alone now and wondered how I would ever get along. Just then I remembered what Father had told me. He said that if anything should ever happen to him, I would be fine. He told me that I knew all he knew about the woods. I knew about the pit and the flint, to keep me warm, give me light and cook the food. I knew how to fish and trap, I knew how to use a sling and how to use a bow. And with the cave I had a secure home, safe from any one, and any thing that might harm me.

I finally drifted off.

Chapter 8
I AM ALONE

I awoke early the next morning. The fire had gone out and it was cold. I remembered all that had happened since two evenings ago, and the fearful thoughts of being alone came back. I crawled out of the bed and put on the skins and boots that Father had made for me. I reached for my rabbit skin coat, but didn't put it on until I was outside the cave. The hole was too small to go through with the coat on. I was then about the same size as Father. I remembered Father's knife in the cave, and took my coat off again to return and get it.

I crawled back in and found the knife next to the pit where I had laid it the night before. I would always have it with me now, like Father had done. When I left the cave, I put on my coat and walked to the bear carcass.

When I got there, I saw the that cub was still beside its slain mother. As I approached, the little cub was frightened and ambled away into the brush, just a little out of sight. It was alone, like myself.

Once again, deep sadness overcame me. I was sad for Father, for me, the little cub, and even the dead bear. What a waste! Why did this all have to happen? If only I had not found the blueberries, or perhaps if I had not gone back to get Father, none of this would have happened.

I shook these thoughts from my head, and the tears from my eyes, then plunged the knife into the bear. Her body was stiff, and the blood had congealed. I thought, at least I would not get the bear's blood all over me. Using a large branch and a stone as a lever, I rolled the solid bear over and started cutting her chest, all the way down to her hind legs. That was how Father skinned deer.

As I looked right into the bear's face, I thought again of the cub. Where is he? I looked about, then realized he was sitting just a few paces behind me. Would this never end? I wished I could get the bear skin and go back home and be done with this tragic scene. I had not eaten anything since two days ago, when Father was still alive.

As I started to cut and peel the hide off the bear, the cub moved closer. I just continued my work. I knew that I needed the hide. I would make a coat out of it once I stretched and dried it. I finally got the hide all the way off, folded it twice, then carried it away on my shoulders, leaving the orphaned cub behind.

When I got back, I dropped the hide down the hole to the cave. I felt very faint and realized I must immediately eat and drink. I staggered down the hill to the creek and drank with my face in the water, then, with my vision and strength failing, I grasped and crawled my way back to the cave. I went to my food supply in the cave and ate my fill of dried smoked fish and dried berries, then collapsed by the fire pit.

After maybe an hour on the floor, I rose and put new wood on the fire to light my workspace. I stretched out the bear hide and used my father's knife to peel the remaining meat from it. I worked at it until all of the flesh was gone. I laid rocks at the edges to hold it, and there it would remain for the next week.

I thought about how I would make my coat. I lay down on the hide. My head was where the bear's head had been, my arms were where the bear's front legs had been, and my legs were where the bear's hind legs had been. All I had to do was to stitch up where I had cut the bear and I would have a bear hide overcoat to use every winter.

After contemplating my new coat, I ate again, then suddenly felt tired, and I very much wanted to sleep to forget my sadness for a time. I returned to my bed, covered myself well, and went fast to sleep.

I'm not sure how long I slept, but before waking, I was visited by dreams about that cub—strange dreams.

In the final visitation, I thought I was sitting at our table near the fire, and across from me the cub was sitting in a chair like a person, eating smoked fish with a fork. Father was also there, serving us both bowls of fresh blueberries. Father smiled and asked, "How do you like your new brother?"

In the dream my mouth was full and I couldn't

answer, but to my surprise the cub spoke and said, "Very much, Father, thank you!"

I awoke in a great sweat and threw off the furs, breathing very rapidly. But I wasn't sure whether I was still dreaming or awake, as there was no fire-light, and in the darkness I thought I heard the bellows of the cub. The cries were continuous and desperate, as though some spirit mocked my sadness over Father and Mother. In my irritation I hollered for silence and the sounds ceased, leaving me alone.

I noticed faint light coming through the chimney and realized I was indeed awake, but the fire had gone out. Maybe the cries were residue from my dreams. After all, just moments before, I thought a bear cub was talking!

I crawled past the dining table to the wood pile, then delivered a mixed load of kindling and branches to the pit, and with the tinderbox, brought warmth and light again to my spacious and lonely home. Then, after some hesitation, I looked at the dining table and sighed with relief to see no cub sitting in Father's chair.

To my surprise I was hungry again. I took two

flanks of dried fillets from the fish satchel, and seated myself at the dining table. Just as I bit into the fish, I thought I heard it squeal. "Am I *still* dreaming?" I wondered. Then I figured it must have been moisture escaping one of the burning branches in the pit. I shook my head, then bit again, and once more I heard a squeal.

"Stars and stripes!" I exclaimed, as my father once did when a plank hit his shin at our sawmill. I set down my fish and stood up, listening keenly for anything other than myself or the fire.

Then came a hoarse, high-pitched voice, which said, "Heeeeeeey," sending such a chill over my body, and sending me to the right of the fire pit to fetch a ready-made torch.

These torches were green branches with the ends split. Tucked into the splits and wrapped around the ends of the branches, were strips of cloth soaked with rodent fat, which were secured with wire. I lit a torch and ran about the cave, looking around, under, and behind every thing. I searched the wood pile, the shelf of food sacks, even under Mother and Father's bed.

"Hhheee-eeeee-eeeeyyy," came the child-like salutation once again.

I now knew what it was and where it was. The bear cub was at the entrance of the cave after following the scent of its mother's hide. It was bellowing for its mother, and perhaps also smelling my dinner. I thought the poor soul must be dying for want of food, and now it was at my door.

I returned to the sack of smoked fillets and took a large handful—enough to feed myself for a day—then took my torch and crawled on my knees through the tunnel toward the opening. No daylight could be seen as the sorry cub had his head through the hole, but he backed out and ran from the opening as the fire and smoke of my torch approached.

I tossed the half dozen fillets through the hole, then returned to fetch the water bucket. I went to the creek. After drinking I filled the bucket and returned to the cave, setting the bucket outside the entrance. I used three rocks to brace the pail, so the clumsy runt wouldn't upset it. I then went back to the warmth of my hearth.

I wasn't sure if Father would approve of my expenditure of fish for a bear cub, but as I pondered this, I concluded that Jesus would approve. In the scriptures, Jesus said:

> Verily I say unto you, Inasmuch as ye have done it unto one of the least of these my brethren, ye have done it unto me.

It could be argued that a bear cub is not my brother, but he was alone, hungry and suffering. In my state of being, he was the closest thing to brethren I could have. If Jesus approved, surely my father would, too.

Chapter 9
BROTHER BEAR

*T*he following morning I took stock of the home's supplies. In addition to fetching more water, I would need another twenty arm-loads of fresh firewood, and four arm-loads of pine needles and sticks for kindling. I would need to check and reset the traps, and if a warm enough day unfolded, perhaps also catch some fish. If a fat enough rodent should await me in a trap, I could restock the torches.

Summer was beginning, and many varieties of berries were ripe. I looked forward to eating berries again and drying them for next winter.

As I completed my many errands in and out of the cave, I recognized that I failed to accurately take account of my food supply. I suppose I wished to not worry about feeding the bear cub, as he was sure to return soon. Acquiring food for myself and a cub wouldn't be much more of a task than it had been for my family of three, but cubs soon become bears, and then how much effort would be required?

By evening I had finished my chores. Father had set a deadfall trap, which is a propped boulder with a trigger made from notched sticks. It had killed and held a coon. I sat by the fire and prepared its pelt for later craft or trade. The meat I set outside for the cub. Glad as I was for the trap's success, I didn't reset it. In this time of loss, I not only fed an orphaned cub, but I did not want to harm any other beings.

That night I had another strange dream. In this one, I was wearing the bear coat, and my hands and feet were natural bear paws. In the valley I overturned a large rock, and there, beneath it was the crushed raccoon, which the cub and I shared.

The next morning I awoke to find the raccoon carcass had been eaten to the bone. By the cave opening were the cub's droppings. I couldn't allow the entrance to my home to become a waste field, so I relocated the skeleton and dung to the appointed mound Father had created behind the large magnolia tree down the hill.

It was confounding that I still dreamt of that cub! I almost feared going to bed each night because I could be certain the cub awaited me behind closed eyelids. Sure as the rising sun, I dreamt again and again. I knew it was my conscience, but I didn't wish to be foolish. Father and Mother always told me to avoid bears and never take any chances with them, and, Lord knows, I had seen with greatest horror, what a bear can do to even a strong and skillful man.

That night I prayed for guidance. "Lord, please take these dreams from me. Show me clearly what I must do. And, please, tell Mother and Father that I love them."

As I took to my bed, I believed my prayer would be answered, and I was eager for it. In the morning I would finally make the bearskin coat.

However, my night was not easy. I had fits that woke me often and heard voices and sounds. Twice I rose and lit a torch, only to return to bed confused and unsettled. To calm myself, I thought about Mother.

Finally, I felt at ease in my bed and in a vision

beheld my dear mother. She was in a white dress and sitting on a rock.

"Mother, are you happy?" I called.

"Yes, Dear," she smiled.

"Where is Father?"

"He is waiting for us at the table."

"Oh," I gasped. "Let us not keep him waiting!"

She rose and took my hand and led me into a cave entrance—a large entrance that we could easily pass through. Inside was a great hall lit with many torches. It was much like my home, but larger, with finer furnishings, and two fire pits. Between them a fountain of fresh water gurgled from a rock and flowed to a pond on the far end of the cave. I knew for certain this was a holy dwelling. Between the hearths and bridging the stream was a most royal table.

"Sit here," Mother said softly.

I sat in a gilded* chair.

Mother said, "I love you, James," then turned and walked across the flowing stream and seated herself at the other end of the table. Across from her I saw Father, and at the head of the table was a man, shining like the sun. I could not look at him. I knew it was the Almighty, who now protects and comforts my departed parents.

Trying to look upon only Mother and Father, I then noticed others were seated on the other side of the stream. On Mother's side, in a chair of wood, and not gold, was an eerie fellow in rags.

"Who is that?" I asked.

"Why, that is Captain Thomas Forrest, of course," said a deep voice from someone sitting across from the Captain. I looked to see who spoke, and there, in a grand chair of blossoming vines, was the great she-bear, and before her a golden platter of apple-sized blueberries.

"Hu—hullo, Bear," I said with surprise.

The bear placed her paws on the table and turned her face toward me. "Hello, James," she replied. "Please, tell me, are you protecting and taking care of my precious cub?"

I couldn't think directly what to answer. Was I taking care of her cub? Yes. Yes, I had fed him. I hurriedly reported, "I fed him dried fish—about six or seven shiners. I also gave him water and a skinned raccoon."

"Where is he?" she asked with worry.

"I ... I don't know."

"Why didn't you bring him?" she asked with greater anxiety.

I looked across the table from my setting, and there on the other side was the back of a gilded chair, and on it was carved the likeness of the little cub.

"Why didn't you bring him!" the she-bear bellowed, now with anguish, sounding very much like Father when he cried over Mother's body.

I suddenly felt I didn't belong at this table without the cub. I turned to run out of the majestic cave to find the cub, but at the mouth of the cave, my foot kicked a stick, which released a great branch that held up the lintel stone over the opening. The stone crushed me beneath its weight, and I awoke on the floor beside my bed in the pitch black of my cave.

Sweaty and shaking, I crawled once more to the fire pit and found the tinderbox and kindling. As I prepared to light the fire, I heard a soft swiping sound. Footsteps?

"Mother?" I asked with trembling voice.

The swiping sounds continued, and they sounded very near.

I feared I was still in my nightmare. I struck the flint, praying I would not behold some horrible vision with the coming light. As the sparks ignited the fuel and the kindling flared, I turned to see what or who was with me inside my cave home.

At the dining table a figure was seated. It looked up at the fire and at me. It was a bear!

I had been inhaling since the ignition, and when the bear's eyes shone at mine, my mouth flew wide open and I screamed all that air through my throat producing a sound like none I had ever made in my life before or since.

The seated bear reeled back and fell off its chair. With the fire grown larger, I could see the intruder was only half as large as the chair. It was just the cub. He had squeezed through the opening of the cave and found his way by scent to the sack of dried fish I had left on the table.

Panting, and with my heart still in my throat, I declared, "Your timing is awful, young bear! The sight of you at my table nearly scared me to heaven!"

The cub belched and licked his fish-crumbed muzzle, cowering behind the chairs.

I snatched the fish satchel and looked inside. He hadn't eaten much. Maybe only three fillets. I took a fourth and sat down on the dirt. "Come and eat, Brother Bear," I said. "I'm sorry I frightened you so."

The bear waited, then sniffed. He knew I had the fish. From his keen nose he also had to know this was my cave, and that the scent of his mother's fur was here, too. He righted himself on his paws and approached me.

"Here, Bear," I said, holding out the fish, then dropping it before him. As he ate, I could see he was covered in dirt from digging at the mouth of the tunnel.

When I returned to bed, I slept with tremendous peace, and never again did I dream of cubs or she-bears at banquet tables.

I awoke to sunlight coming down the chimney. I checked the cave entrance and saw the rake marks where Brother Bear had enlarged the opening. The noonday sun was above the magnolia. "Time to make my coat," I said.

I lit the fire pit again and found the cub where he ought to be—lying in the middle of his mother's stretched hide.

"Wake up, Brother Bear," I said, touching his nose.

The cub's eyes opened, and he showed no fear of me at all. In fact, he crawled across the fur and placed his head on my lap. Perhaps the young cub, having been reunited with his mother's scent and good food, associated me with his mother.

"Just wait until you see me in my new coat!"

I trimmed the hide, cut little holes along the edges, and used knotted strips of hide to gather them. I finished the edges with a lapping stitch. I even had a hood where the neck had been. I stitched the top in such a fashion so when raised, only my face would be exposed. I had made bone buttons two days prior, and I stepped into the bear suit before latching them. It fit loosely, but very well over body, arms and legs. I must have looked more bear than man! I liked my new coat very much. In celebration I growled loudly.

A squeal sounded behind me.

I turned to see the little cub. He had been asleep on my bed while I worked, and I had forgotten him. I just stood there, dressed in his mother's hide. The cub looked at me and I looked at the cub. I wondered what the small creature thought as he beheld me in the dim fire light.

The cub approached me and squealed again, sniffing my legs, then he rubbed his face against them.

"Who do you think I am, Little Bear?" I asked.

After thoroughly smelling me, the cub remained beside me, as though he expected me to do something.

It was time to try the coat in the outdoors. I took it off and carried it and my pack with me through the tunnel. Even though the cub had widened the opening, it was still too small to pass through wearing the hide. Outside, I put the coat on, then my deerskin boots. The cub appeared at my side, and as I walked he followed me, just as all young creatures follow their mothers.

On the south face of a hill, at the edge of our property, was a cluster of fruiting bushes Father and I had planted many years ago, and I knew the berries would be ripe. Once there, I started to pick and eat them. So did the cub.

Father had taught me to never eat berries when they're white. Some berries, like mulberries, can make one feverish if eaten white or unripe. I pointed at the black and red ones on the twigs, and the cub followed my finger and ate.

I was glad to see the cub eating something other than the last of my dried fish stores. The berries would be plentiful this year, and I knew we would come here often. We ate all the ripe berries we found, thus none were gathered for drying. It was too warm to continue wearing heavy fur, so I shed my bear skin and carried it.

I walked on to survey the property, and dutifully the cub followed, even though I was no longer clad in his mother's hide. I had become the bear cub's new mother!

Chapter 10
GREAT ROOM

By late summer, Bear had gotten much bigger. In fact, we had to widen the cave opening again. This was not the exhausting task I first imagined.

As I began to dig, Bear began to dig. The digging power of a bear should not be underestimated. Soon my task was simply to carry away the clawed clay and stone. With the much larger opening, it fell to me to construct a door, otherwise all manner of beasts would make our home theirs. Mice and rats had always passed through, but they bothered us little, and mostly made for the small hole on the far side of our cave.

The door was an oval, hide-hinged trap of cedar. I fastened brush and moss to it, which made it near impossible to identify, but Bear had no problem as he followed scent more than sight.

This door did not last long, and not owing to poor construction. I once shut myself inside to clean, thinking Bear would be content to explore and forage. He complained at the door, but I did not open it. I continued sweeping his shed fur into a pile, then heard a crash unlike anything I'd ever heard in our quiet cave home.

I knew right away it was the destruction of my well-crafted trap door and that Bear was not one to be shut out. I then had to build a better door, this time of walnut, a wood that dulls the craftsman faster than his tools. The new door was larger, heavier, stronger, and affixed by holes bored into stone. Still, I knew I must train Bear not to wreck the door. He was not patient by nature.

I was both Father and Mother to this creature, and it fell to me to train him, just as my father and mother trained me. I had already taught him to eat within the cave only when and what I appointed. I also trained Bear to stop getting on my bed. This was needful because he would soon crush it. Bear claimed an unused space between the table and the fire pit, and would scratch the earth and roll before sleeping. While I read, he would gnaw his claws to clean them, and sometimes sniff along the rat trail that led to the hole on the far wall.

With Bear in the home, rodents made themselves scarce. Perhaps he caught a few. He is most playful, and reminds me of the puppies I have read about in Mother's old books and the ones I saw playing in the streets when Father took me to Blairsville.

I made a ball of skins and taught him to fetch it when thrown. He could never resist the temptation to pull it apart when I wasn't minding him. The ball got smaller daily, even though I kept stitching it back up. He also chewed my deer hide pants so terribly that I needed to find and fell a buck to make new ones. My leather supply was low, and I knew Bear must crave more than fruit and fish.

Bear fully believed I was his parent, and I admit I stopped thinking of him as just an animal. I came to love his face, his sounds, and his funny ways. He was *my* bear. Perhaps, in another year or two, he would be even larger than his mother had been, which was the largest black bear I had ever seen.

It was hard to foresee living with him when he got that big, but I thought that perhaps he would "leave the nest" at the appropriate time, as God's creatures tend to do. But, I realized, until then, he was mine and I was his, and I no longer felt alone.

Bear's habit of sniffing and scratching at the back wall was increasing. Often I'd tell him to stop and go to his spot (he learned to obey many spoken commands). Then one night, he hurled his weight against the wall and created an awful rumble, and a stone fell from high on that wall. It troubled me that a portion of our home might not be stable.

I stepped outside to relieve myself. When I returned, I threw new brush and logs on the fire to begin my reading. But as I sat at the table, I noticed Bear was not in his place. I looked at my bed and he wasn't there, either. Then I realized Bear was gone! He hadn't passed me to go through the tunnel. How could he have disappeared?

"Bear!" I called.

"Bear," a voice answered.

This gave me a chill much like I experienced when I woke from a nightmare to see a bear at my table.

"Who's there?" I asked with what I hoped was a bold voice.

"There," it answered softly.

I lit a torch and walked hesitantly to the back wall. There was a pile of rubble and a large hole where the wall had collapsed. The hole was wider than my armspan and almost as high as my head. Bear had broken through the cave wall, but not to the outside. I hoped he was not injured. Flowing water must have made a cavity beside the one we had been living in, and this is where the rodents had been going. But the space I beheld was not a rat's nest or rabbit's warren.* It was a vestibule that opened into a much larger room—*much* larger. My torch light didn't even illuminate the other side of the chamber.

I heard splashing and knew Bear was in water. It was an underground pond! I walked farther into the room to explore what Bear had found.

The pond was about 150 feet long and about 30 to 60 feet wide. The rest of the room was more than double the area of the pond. The floor was mostly rock and the walls were solid rock, about 40 feet high, and higher in some parts. The water reflected the torchlight, and as I made my presence known I could hear the rats and mice fleeing.

Bear was enjoying his bath. The torch could burn several minutes more, so I propped it in a cleft rock and took off my boots and hides to splash and swim with Bear. The water was cold, though not as cold as a stream. It felt wonderful.

When I called again to Bear, I heard my voice say "Bear," a second time. Bear looked to the back of the cave from whence the echo came. I held still and silent then shouted "Bear!" again, so Bear could observe the echo.

Bear growled and the cave growled back. This startled Bear who growled even louder, and the cave growled back again. Bear climbed out of the water and stood between me and the back of the cave in a most threatening posture and growled again. He thought there was another bear, and Bear was ready to protect me.

"Don't fret, Bear," I said and stroked his shoulder, but he remained like a statue, opening his mouth and showing his teeth to the far, dark end of the cavern, sniffing intently.

I returned to swimming. I could not swim very well, but the water wasn't very deep near where I placed the torch, so I just stayed in that area. As the flame began to wane, I got out of the water and gathered my clothes. "Come, Bear," I said, and began to walk toward the breach.

Bear was still growling at his echo.

"Bear!" I said, sternly.

Bear obeyed and followed after me. As we came to the breach he shook himself, sending water in all directions. I was glad he did that before we were near our bedding.

After a while, I redressed to explore the new expanse of the cavern. I took about a dozen candles of fat oil. These were hand-sized rocks with holes most of the way through, which Father and I had bored and filled with fat. We made wicks from dried strips of hardwood. These candles could burn for many hours.

Once we had used these for reading, but as I no longer trapped and hunted often enough to keep a supply of animal fat, I now read by wood fire and saved the candles for special occasions. I would light these candles with the torch and place them along my journey through the new cave room, then fetch them on my way back, thereby not getting lost in the dark.

I told Bear to stay, and he made me proud by obeying. I used my biggest torch to light my way. As I walked I could see little bright spots in the walls that shone like stars, but most of them were up higher than I could reach. Then, as I examined the farthest quarter of the long room, I found a big shiny spot that stretched about twenty feet long, and was as wide as a foot. I held the torch up to it and could see it was yellow and in some places greenish.

I recalled Father speaking about gold being in *veins* in the earth. Then I thought of Mother telling me about a pot of gold. I didn't need to chase a rainbow—this mountain home *was* a pot of gold! The gold in the walls of this cave would fill much, much more than just a pot.

There were holes and recesses in the walls higher than I could reach. It would be difficult to fully explore the entire cave in a single day, and I realized that perhaps there was much of it I'd never see. I was most delighted that Bear and I had such an abundance of fresh water—no more running to the creek with buckets in all sorts of weather.

I returned, gathering candles, and found Bear sitting dutifully where I put him. "Good boy," I said, rubbing his head. "We've got gold, Bear!" I continued in a hush, "Whatever you do, don't tell anyone."

Bear looked at me with resolve, then mumbled a bear word, as though he knew what I just said and agreed. I'd like to think he did, but how would a bear ever know what gold was, or what sounds a human would make in speaking of it? I pondered the other ways we communicate with the rest of Nature, and how Nature communicates with us.

Bear was indeed intelligent. Even though he was being raised by a human instead of a mother bear, he had good instincts. Often, when we went exploring outdoors, he would insist on going a different direction than I, and time after time it would be a shortcut to home or one of our favorite places. He helped me find food and dead animals to skin, even before they stank.

I knew plenty of things a bear wouldn't know and helped him in ways no bear could, but he knew and sensed many things I never would, and it helped me mightily.

Bear was even helpful with fishing! Even with all the water in our cave we still had to return to the creek for fish. Also, there was just something about the creek that made Bear want to play. Cold weather would be coming soon, and I realized that I needed to start catching and smoking fish—perhaps more fish than ever with Bear growing so fast.

As I began to catch fish and put them in a basket, Bear watched me with fascination. Then he ran upstream on his own. I heard a splash, and seconds later, Bear returned with a fish in his mouth, which he dropped in the grass beside my basket. He was doing what I was doing!

"You are a fisher bear!" I told him. He seemed very proud of himself.

I need not have worried about running out of food over the coming winter. The nut trees had produced enough that autumn to feed a multitude. Although Father had taught me how to boil and soak the tannin from acorns, that autumn I had no need to go through the process of making the bitter nuts more palatable, because the pecans, walnuts, and almonds were so plentiful. I did boil enough acorns to replenish my supply of tannin water, which Father taught me was good to clean cuts and scrapes and take the sting out of insect bites.

We had more dried berries than I'd ever seen in one place and we had root and leaf vegetables, too. By the equinox I had two large sacks of fish, eight large sacks of roots, ten large sacks of nuts—pecans, almonds, black walnuts—and six small sacks of dried fruits. Since Bear did not seem to mind the bitterness, we also had two large sacks of acorns for him to enjoy.

Bear and I ate our fill of berries that summer and autumn, and there was still plenty for the other animals that shared our land. The peach and apple trees Father had planted when I was a child were bursting with ripe fruit. These I couldn't dry very well, but Bear and I ate them until we were stuffed. Bear would even sit on his hind and hold a peach between his front paws—just like a person—mindful to not eat the pit. He ate the little apples whole.

I would continue fishing and gathering to add to our stocks until it was too cold to do so. I was pleased to not hunt and trap anymore. It was more than a single person's work to kill, skin, clean and smoke a large animal in the warm seasons and it had to be done quickly to prevent spoilage or insects.

Since Father was killed, the only hunting I had done was when I killed a buck. The dying minutes of that buck still troubled my conscience.

Now that Bear could help me find animals that recently died from falls, copperhead strikes, fights or disease, our supply of pelts was plentiful. I had coon, beaver, duck, possum, squirrel, raven, owl, snake, rabbit, and fawn. Bear even brought me turtle shells, which I cleaned and for which I found sundry* uses.

After a few good days of fishing and gathering, I determined it was time for a harvest celebration. We had been eating fresh fruit, nuts and berries for months and it was time for something cooked. I lit the pit and started making up a banquet.

I put fish, potatoes, carrots, and onions in the smoker. I had found rosemary and sage, which seasoned the stew nicely. I ground some pecans and almonds into a paste, and wrapped it in greens, making nutmeat dumplings. This would be a feast for me and Bear. Father would have said "Jolly good eating."

As I set the table, I suddenly felt a terrible sorrow. I missed Father and Mother. I remembered a Christmas feast Mother prepared, which was one of the happiest memories I had. I no longer knew when Christmas was, except that it usually came before the snow.

Father and the almanac showed me how to find the equinoxes by the position of the sun as it rises each morning. I had to stand on the ridge above the cave to see it.

Most of the time I don't know what month it is, and never do I know the time of day. Father had a timepiece, but it stopped long ago. I know there are 24 hours in a day, 7 days in a week, and 12 months in a year, but that's not as helpful as knowing seasons, when to plant and when to harvest. Since Mother and Father died, I haven't had holidays. I missed holidays, I missed Mother and Father, and I missed having people answer me in my own language.

Then I had an idea that might seem crazy to most people—people who don't live alone with a Bear—I got two small, empty sacks and drew faces on them with charcoal. I stuffed them with pelts and tied them off. I ran outside and fetched pine, ivy and moss and filled two large sacks. I placed these in chairs and fitted one with Mother's dress and the other with Father's extra shirt. I placed the heads on them and topped them with Mother's and Father's hats.

Now I could imagine I had human company. I poured bowls of stew and set them before my guests along with two nut rolls.

Bear was no longer allowed to get on chairs or set his paws on the table. He had his own special woven straw mat. I filled the water bucket half full with stew and admonished Bear to be careful with it. I placed stones around it so he wouldn't knock it over. Lastly, I seated myself and said grace.

I talked to our guests and listened keenly as they

told me about their travels. I got quite caught up in this. I explained to them that life with a bear was quite agreeable. As I did so, I realized how strange I was behaving, talking to canvas sacks.

I wanted to cry again, but then I said, "James, you do have a good life! You have food, you have land, you even have a mountain of gold! No sense in being sad over Mother and Father anymore. It's something that you can not change." I put away Mother's and Father's clothes and emptied the sacks.

I was surely glad that I had Bear, but I wondered if he would hurt a person. After all, his mother killed my father. I guessed that if Bear did not know a man he would likely kill him if he was intent on protecting me.

He had eaten his whole bucket of stew, so I poured into the bucket the two bowls I had served our guests, which he greatly enjoyed.

I thought again about the gold in the cave. I took the candles and tinderbox and made for the big room. I placed a candle every ten paces until all the candles were arrayed, but much of the great room was left to be seen. I fetched my torches and filled a skin with stones, hickory branches and kindling. I returned to the farthest candle, took ten more paces and set up a torch. (This was where I had stopped when I last explored.) I went farther and placed another torch. The ground disappeared into water. I could see it wasn't deep, and I waded through it for about twenty feet, keeping my supplies on my shoulder.

Continuing, I came onto solid rock and found the end of the room. The tall stone walls came together in a vee, and there the colorful, shiny veins were most plentiful. I placed another torch, then built a fire pit.

When the hickory fire was crackling, I extinguished my torch to save it for my return. I knew the other torches would burn out before my trek back.

I lay on my back and beheld the sparkling walls as they reflected the dancing light. It was a beautiful place, a holy place, I thought. Surely, I had the biggest and the most majestic home that anyone could ever have. It was a secret mansion inside the earth. I thought it must be a bit like heaven—the kind of place where my mother and father would surely be.

Yes, this must be what Jesus was talking about when he said, "Thy will be done in earth as it is in heaven."

I remembered how precious Father and Mother said gold was to regular people. If people knew this gold was here, hundreds of people would come to this cave and probably fight over it. They would destroy these walls with picks and hammers. They would fill the pond with rubble. They would cut down the woods and level the hills for roads and buildings. Animals would be forced to find new homes, like the Indians had to do. Lovers of gold would destroy heaven on earth.

Chapter 11
THE STORM

*T*hat winter we had most unusual weather. It became warm for a few days, then one night it started raining and thundering. For the first time in the cave, I could hear the winds whistling through the chimney and see the flashing light through it, even with a fire burning. The wind was monstrous, and somehow blew the trap door upside-down. I went to the entrance to pull it shut. There was a most hideous roar and my ears popped. Trees had been twisted clean from the ground, and branches and soil were flying sideways. It took all my strength to pull the door fast.

Inside the cave, the burning logs and ashes had scattered and the chairs had overturned. I had to use a possum skin to pick up the many embers before they harmed our furnishings. I could see Bear was frightened. I wondered about wind strong enough to terrify a bear in a cave.

The night became more peculiar. Water began to trickle down the rock walls. I had never seen anything like this before. I lit two torches, thinking that perhaps we should flee to the larger room. Just then watery mud began to fall through our chimney and the fire pit went out. I heard a loud slap on the ground behind me. A stone had fallen from above! A couple more fell and Bear started for the great room. I was scared, too, and I followed Bear with the torches.

In the great room the waters of the pond were higher, and the surface was moving and bubbling. Then I realized I was hearing squeals. It was rats! Rats were coming up out of the water! About fifty or sixty rats came to the ground near us and then ran to a different part of dry ground.

A minute later, I saw snakes come out of the water, and they turned from us and joined the rats. The rats weren't running from the snakes and the snakes weren't eating the rats. They seemed to be waiting together for the storm to stop. I thought of the Bible's story of Noah, and how animals had all come to the ark on their own. Even Bear didn't mind the hordes of creatures sharing our space. He seemed to know we all wanted to survive this awful storm and needed to overlook natural predatory instincts to do so.

Water was coming down the rocks in the great room, too. A very large stone fell into the pond, and small rocks and soil fell upon me and Bear. Bear shook the dirt from his neck, and I could see traces of gold shining in his fur. I put my hand through my hair, then looked at my palm and saw yellow glimmering in the mud.

Gold was raining on my head!

I heard another loud crash in the pond, and a wall of water splashed every creature and the torches went out, leaving us in complete darkness.

I wished that the storm would stop! Bear could not help me if the walls were going to cave in, but I held him close. All I could do was pray to God that he not let this happen.

When the storm stopped, I thought God had heard me and saved us. I felt my way back into my home and found the tinderbox, candles, and a fresh torch. There was water and mud all over the floor, but not many stones had fallen.

Water and mud had fallen on the satchel that contained my writings. This, my life's story, had several pages where the ink smeared, and I had to (at a later time) use fresh paper to rewrite many pages.

I was grateful that our home had not been destroyed, but I knew I would need to repair the chimney. I also realized I must find a safe container for my writings, otherwise they could be ruined by some chance happening.

I hadn't troubled my mother's things since her death, but she had a fine, wooden spice box just the right size for my papers.

I returned to the great room and saw Bear and all the smaller creatures. "We are safe now," I told Bear. I tried to lead him back to the house, but he would not get up. He still seemed scared. Then it started all over again—wind, rain, and once more rocks began to fall.

"Oh, God, where are you?" I cried. "I really need you now. Please, please help me!" I knelt beside Bear and wondered if this was the night we would die, and if we would become a feast for rats and mice.

As I held Bear I could feel him trembling. I stopped worrying about myself and sought to comfort him. "It's all right, Bear," I said. "All creatures die. Maybe this is our time, and maybe not. It does no good to fear. I have had a wonderful and happy life. I have been loved by wonderful people and you. You have had happiness and love, too. Don't fear. If God gives us more time, good. If it's time to go to heaven, it's just like this place, but even better."

Even though I was speaking to calm Bear, I realized I was right: there is no point in fearing death. My fear was not helping Bear, and I knew that being fearless and grateful was the best way to keep Bear and myself happy.

Bear stopped trembling, then yawned. And soon the winds and the rain stopped. I wondered if the storm was supposed to teach me about fear, the way Jesus taught Peter on the stormy sea. I started walking Bear back inside the smaller room, and I looked up and said, "Thank you, God, thank you."

Then I added, "And if that wasn't a lesson for me, thank you just the same."

Morning light was coming through the damaged chimney hole. Bear and I went outside and saw many trees lying on their sides, their roots torn from the ground. The sky was clearing, and there was a double rainbow.

"No need to run to the find a pot of gold," I told Bear. "We have a mountain full."

Bear and I had much to do. Cold weather was returning. There would be debris to clear from our gardens and orchards, a chimney to repair, and of a certain, newly killed animals for Bear to find to keep our pelt and fat supplies high. Each find would be fresh meat for Bear.

What troubled me most were the snakes that found their way into the cave. I had seen rats and mice, but never snakes. Water must have flooded the hidden rat nests and snake tunnels, and they knew to swim through the water to safety. In the storm I had forgotten to notice the markings on the snakes.

I determined that I must wear the knife and carry a garden hoe.

Father and I had killed many copperheads and rattle snakes in years past. I kept a fire burning near the breach, so the warmth would attract snakes. I killed every poisonous snake that appeared, including two moccasins, three copperheads, and two rattlers, including a very tiny one. Father used to say that it was not the size, it was the poison.

I collected nine snake skins, and Bear got to eat plenty of snake. This meat and the several animals found after the storm fed Bear well and helped our supply of nuts and dried foods last longer. I hadn't eaten animal flesh in many months, so I had some smoked rattler and venison.

More rains came, and then snow, but our cave did not leak again like the night of the big storm. The breaches the wind and water created that night must have settled and filled with clay. The rats and snakes must have found new homes out of our sight, and for the rest of the winter the cave was peaceful.

Chapter 12
ENCOUNTERS

Father taught me that bears take a long sleep in the coldest part of winter, then come out of their dens hungry and thinner than before. Bear did sleep a lot in the long, cold nights of winter, but our cave was comfortable and he was awake every day to eat and empty his wastes outside the cave. Instead of becoming skinny, Bear ate very well all winter and grew very large. He was now much heavier than I, and when he stood his head was higher than mine.

When the vernal equinox came, I was glad that spring was returning. I was asleep in my bed and Bear got up. I thought he was going outside in order to keep our home clean, but he just stood facing the tunnel, sniffing.

"Do you smell the flowers blooming?" I asked him.

Bear's posture became threatening. Something was alarmimg him. He began to growl louder than I'd ever heard him, and I threw off my cover.

"What is it, Bear?" I asked, starting to get up from my bed.

Suddenly Bear charged through the tunnel, running so hard that his much larger body smote* the walls and sent clay and rock falling. He struck the trap door wide open and vanished into the light.

"Bear!" I shouted, running after him. As I came to the opening I saw two black bears in a fierce battle, and one was much larger. For a second, I didn't know which was Bear.

I stood by the trap, holding the handle, ready to shut it if necessary. I was glad I had built this heavier door of walnut and fastened it to stone, otherwise Bear would have destroyed it. I hoped he had not crushed his head when he struck it. I pondered if his head was unharmed, how mighty is a bear's skull!

But my thoughts of the door were only fleeting. The bears roared and collided, and the bigger bear pushed the other down the mountain until it fled. The big bear chased it out of sight.

What had happened? Was my dear Bear injured or dying? Would he return? Would a strange and hungry bear be at my door wanting me and my stores for food? I hoped I could protect myself with fire, so I hurried to light two torches and returned to my door.

I didn't have to stand guard long. A bear came limping back, and I recognized my friend. I almost cried for joy. "Come, Bear," I called. He hobbled back inside, and I shut the trap behind him.

Blood covered Bear's entire head, and some was on his shoulder and side. It was difficult to discover where it had come from. Was it all his? It took some time, but I saw his face had been clawed and his shoulder bitten deeply. There was a lump on his head between his eyes. Much of the blood had to be from the other bear.

I realized that Bear was now now bigger than other adult bears. He had attacked the strange bear to protect his home and me. I was still shaking from witnessing the power and ferocity that Bear had displayed. It conjured the horror of my Father's tragic slaying. I had managed to not recall that day for so long. I had to banish my terror and sorrows, because Bear was hurt and needed my help.

I took Bear to the great room and washed his wounds in the pond. I thought at first to use Father's extra shirt as a bandage, but straightway realized I could not stand to see blood on my father's clothes and a bear in the same place again. I took Mother's dress instead and returned to tend the gushing tear on Bear's shoulder. I pressed the cotton dress into the gash. Bear growled in protest, but he seemed to know I was helping him.

The blood continued oozing, and I wondered what else I could do to stop it. I remembered Father telling me ice could slow down bleeding, and there were still patches of melting snow scattered on the mountain. "Stay, Bear," I said, then ran outside with the dress. I looked about, but the other bear had not returned. I wondered if Bear had killed the intruder. I filled the dress with what little snow remained in shady places.

Soon I was back with Bear, holding the snow-packed dress against his shoulder. My hands began to ache from the cold. I tightly tied the sleeves around Bear's arm. Soon he lay down on his other side on the smooth rock beside the pond. The bleeding had stopped.

"You protected me, Bear. I love you." Yes, I truly loved him. He had saved our home from a hungry, wild bear. He had met his own kind, and he was now an adult. I didn't believe he would remain with me much longer, but I didn't want him to go. He was a noble and beautiful creature, and he was my best friend in the world.

"I love you, Bear," I repeated.

He looked up at me, then closed his eyes with a deep sigh.

Twice every day, I would clean Bear's wounds and wrap them in dry cloth, using all the woven cloth we had, including Father's shirt. I even bandaged Bear's clawed face. On the fourth day, I approached Bear with bandages, and he growled at me and backed away. He was tired of being nursed.

"It's all right, Bear," I said, then put the stained clothes down.

Bear understood when I said, "All right, Bear." Those were the words that meant danger was gone, or that he should be calm. I had been saying it to him since he was a cub, and I knew he really understood those words the night of the big storm.

When Bear's flesh had closed, it was time to tend our fruit trees and berry bushes, then start fishing the streams again. Spring had arrived, and we still had nuts and potatoes left from November.

The big storm had rearranged our land somewhat, with several trees on their sides with roots displayed. Runoff had filled the creek and sent the waters in a new path. Fish hadn't swum this far inland yet, so Bear and I would have to find a new place to catch fish. I knew there was another stream west of our home, as I had jumped over it years ago when I chased the rainbow.

When we found the neighboring stream, I was surprised at how much bigger it was. Right away Bear jumped in and caught a fish. I cheered for him and opened the basket, but instead of bringing the fish, Bear ate it. He also ate the next one he caught. I placed my fishes in the basket, but Bear had nothing to do with it. He played on his own, rolled on sunlit grass, scratched on trees, and investigated many scents while I fished. I called him occasionally, but he didn't come. I wondered if Bear would soon decide to live without me.

Finally, I began to walk home with a basket of fish, but no Bear. Surely, he could follow my scent, and certainly the scent of a basket of fish. For that matter, I realized that any bear could follow the scent, so I hastened* my steps toward home.

"We greet you!" came a voice.

I stopped and spun around, wondering what I had just heard. I hadn't heard a human voice for so long, and was half-convinced it was my own mind.

"You are Mark?" asked the voice.

I looked up the hill and saw four men, Indians—Cherokee, I guessed. I realized I had been asked a question. "I am James," I replied.

Two of the men held bows with arrows nocked.* The men spoke amongst* themselves with words I couldn't understand. The one who spoke to me before spoke again, "Is this your land?"

I didn't know if I was still on Father's property. He taught me its boundaries when I was quite young, and I didn't recall the western edge, and some places seemed unfamiliar after the storm.

"I don't know," I answered.

"At last, a White man who isn't sure this land is his!" the speaker laughed, but with the sound of irritation.

"Friend!" I called to them.

Suddenly the man crouched with alarm. I feared they were about to shoot their arrows at me, but a crashing sound behind me revealed why they took cover—Bear!

Bear was charging from behind me in their direction.

I hollered, "Bear, stay!"

Bear stopped in two strides, but remained between me and the strangers, growling.

"It's all right, Bear," I said. "It's all right."

Bear stopped growling.

"Come, Bear."

Bear turned back and stayed at my side.

"Good boy, Bear."

The startled Indians slowly stood up.

"Friend," I repeated.

All four Indians turned the palms of their hands

upward, then looked to the sky.

"My bear will not hurt you," I declared, hoping it was true, "if you do not hurt me."

"That is a good thing," said the English-speaking Indian. He stepped forward cautiously. "Do you prefer bears to other White men?"

"I do not know any White men," I said. "I live alone with this bear."

"I was told this land was given to a White man named Mark," the Indian said, then pointed, "and land over there to a Donald, and other Cherokee land to other White men."

I nodded. "Mark was my father, and he is dead."

The man stood before me—the first human male I had ever seen here other than my father. He smiled in wonder at the bear standing by my shoulder, then at the hand-made deerskin clothing I wore. "A great friend you have. You see differently than other White man. You do not have their madness."

"All I know is this land," I said.

The man sighed and said, "All I know is this land." The words seemed to burn his throat as he spoke.

I nodded. I remembered that this territory had belonged to the Cherokee Nation, and had been taken from them. Nearly all Indians were removed by force and marched to the West, but a few who lived far from the towns must have been able to remain in the wilds. They were trying to continue their way of living, but without their tribes or the freedom to travel and build as they wished.

"We are sons of the same land," he said. "We are brothers." He seemed older than my father had been. I can only guess he was 40 or more. One of the men with him was about his age, the other two with bows were younger. The man spoke to his companions, perhaps telling them I was their brother. With a bear at my command and moccasins on my feet, they were quick to agree.

They appeared to be hunting. I had a dozen fish and a tinderbox in my pack. I invited them to eat with me. They accepted, and I built a fire in a clearing. I told Bear to go home, and he departed obediently. One Indian had killed two rabbits, so we added his catch to mine, searing them on a slab of slate.

The English-speaking man had a pouch of salt, and for the third time in my life I tasted salted meats. He had lived among the White settlers for many years. He had English-style boots, a leathern belt, and a Bowie knife similar to Father's. I was fascinated to see another such knife, but it was no marvel to him that I should have one.

He told me they were in this territory hunting a badly-injured bear who had left bloody tracks near this stream, and that they needed its fur and meat. Clearly, it was one my bear had fought. I told him my bear had mauled it in my defense.

He said he was called Nathaniel, but his real name was something to do with eagles or hawks. He was much more accustomed to American-style living than I was, but he remarked at how educated I appeared to be. He also said I spoke like an Englishman rather than an American. I told him of my parents, and how they came to live in these mountains just a year after coming from England. He asked why, after my parents' deaths, I didn't move to Blairsville to live with my own kind. I could only say that I felt at home here, though I did get lonesome.

I did not reveal where my cave home was, nor did they ask. They did ask about the empty cabin. I told them they could stay in it if they wished, and that I would write a letter stating so, perchance White men disapproved. The cabin would probably need repairs after a few years of neglect.

Nathaniel the Cherokee accepted my offer of the letter. He said it would not be for himself, but another orphan, someone who needed a White man's kind of home.

I agreed. I told him I would write the letter and leave it in the cabin before the full moon, which was just a few nights coming.

Before we parted, he told me of the many peoples who used to live among these hills. Nathaniel had lived right here, on the east side of the stream I had just fished, about three hills away from the cabin Father and Mother had built. He described how the Cherokee were given a letter from the United States government promising they had these lands forever, but years later, soldiers came and forced them to leave. He said almost half of his tribe died marching in the winter to unknown lands. Because he was educated by Whites, he got a job on a sailing ship in New Orleans. His ship sailed to Charleston, and while at port he abandoned his crewmates and escaped back into the hills of his homeland. His companions were distant relatives he found still hiding in the mountains.

I told him I was so sorry for the wrongful suffering of his people, that I detested the cruelty inflicted upon them, and that I freely shared this land with him if he would continue to share it with me. I promised that, besides whoever resides in the cabin, I would never reveal to White men that I knew Cherokee were still living in these lands.

Nathaniel looked much different than his friends. They were thoroughly painted, not in bold colors, but clay. They seemed to be disguising themselves. What parts of their skin showed were tattooed and much lighter and smoother than Nathaniel's. I knew they did not see much sunlight, and that they probably lived in caves as I did.

When I asked if they had women folk and children, they didn't answer, but instead asked me a peculiar question, "Do you know of this land's treasure?"

"I know," I said, "and it belongs only to the land."

Nathaniel thanked me and I thanked him. I asked him one special favor: for him to teach his companions to recognize my bear—scarred nose and scarred right shoulder—and swear to never kill Bear unless it was in defense. I told him, "You are my brother, and Bear is my brother."

He spoke with his companions and they gestured that they agreed. "We will never hunt Scar Nose Bear."

Chapter 13
WATERFALL

When I returned home, Bear was waiting just inside the trap door. He had learned to raise it with his nose, so he could come and go as he pleased. I had saved morsels of seared rabbit to reward his prior good behavior. I wanted him to know how glad I was that he listened to my voice in the presence of strange beings. Bear ate the reward from my hand, then smelled me for a long time, because I had been with other humans. He followed me inside, where we bedded down. I knew he had been worried about me while he waited. I had never before passed up his company for another.

I couldn't help but wonder how many more months I would share with Bear. I could feel a struggle inside him, between being a brother to me and finding a life of his own.

The next day, I remained indoors with Bear. He was nearly recovered from his fight, but the clothes that had been my parents' were permanently stained by his blood. Though I washed them in ashwater, I could not remove all the stains. I determined that I would try to remedy this by finding red and blue berries to dye them all a solid color, perhaps making them look regal instead of blighted.

That day I had a different mission, which was to write my first letter to another person. I thought long about what I should write, and finally I took Father's quill and some ink I had made from ground berries, fish blood and rust scrapings, and wrote in the manner of the Virginians:

> I, James Hill of North Georgia, do grant asylum, lodging, and generous provision to the persons of Creek or Cherokee blood residing in this cabin, built by my Father and Mother, Mark and Sarah Hill. Duly signed this day by myself, it's rightful inheritor
> . . .

I didn't know what day it was, but I believed it

was sometime in the midst of April, so I wrote "the ides* of April, 1852." I wasn't truly sure of the year, I admit.

Later that day, after the ink had thoroughly dried and set, I took the letter with me along the old creek bed toward the cabin. I invited Bear to come, but half-way there he diverted, following a scent. I continued alone without pausing. I wanted to see the cabin, as I had not set eyes on the place since we left it behind.

As I arrived, I saw that a plank had fallen from the roof, moss grew on the outer walls, and that some of the shutters had been opened. The door was also open, and inside, the floor was muddy from the breach in the roof. The fire pit and chimney were still whole. The book shelf was missing from the wall, as were shutters from the south window. A glass bottle was in one corner. Upon inspection it had a leaf* affixed to one side that read:

Finest
Tennessee Whiskey
from Charred Barrels
Sweet and Good.

I didn't know what the inscription meant, but the odor from the bottle was not agreeable. At first I thought to keep the bottle, for it could serve some purpose, then I realized it was perfect for securing my letter.

I walked back to the old creek bed and filled the bottle half-way with pebbles to make it heavy, then returned to the cabin. There was one wall shelf remaining, where Father used to place his knife each night above his bed. The roof above that spot was still very solid, so it was a good place to leave the letter. I placed the letter on the shelf and set the bottle upon it. Visitors to the cabin would see the bottle and see the note.

As I walked back to the cave along the old creek bed, Bear appeared and walked beside me. His fur was dusted with yellow pollen. He had been amongst our budding fruit trees on the southwest side of the mountain. I could tell he'd had a good time, and as we walked where our creek had been, I got an idea.

"This is a beautiful day," I said to Bear. "I think it will be clear and warm past the morrow. Let's go on holiday to the west creek!"

At the cave I prepared for being away with Bear for two or three days. I set my large deerskin on Bear's mat and rolled them both up. I would give these a needed washing in the creek, dry them in the sun, and afterward we would eat and sleep upon them under the stars. I brought my fishing traps, and in case we had no luck in the stream, I put a plentiful sack of nuts and diced roots in my pack.

When we arrived at the west creek, I asked Bear which way he wanted to go, upstream or downstream. Bear lifted his nose and chose upwind, which was downstream. He was following a scent with great interest. After many minutes I started to hear something—it was nothing like I had ever heard before. We stopped and listened. It was a powerful sound, like a tremendous storm blowing through trees, but only a gentle breeze was blowing.

We walked on, and the sound grew ever louder, and the ground rumbled. I could sense we were approaching some awesome wonder of Nature, and that I would have new thoughts about God.

Ahead of us there were no trees, but sky. The ground was mostly rock. I realized the creek was rushing right over the edge of the rocks. We walked to the edge and looked down to see the stream falling a great distance, spilling over boulders to a pond below. Beyond the pond was a meadow with several deer near the treeline. It was an amazing sight! I had never seen a waterfall higher than my head before, and this one was at least 200 feet!

I pointed at the meadow below to show Bear where I wanted to go. We had to find our way down the cliff. Bear jumped over the creek to its west bank and put his nose down and followed a scent. He had found a deer trail, which took us into the woods and down a steep path lined with big leaf ferns, mossy trees, and high grasses. A deer in the woods saw us coming, a human and a bear, and let out a whistle of alarm. I knew every deer would be gone when we got to the bottom of the trail.

As we walked out on the meadow and looked up at the waterfall, I was moved with the beauty of the place. The cascading water seemed full of life as it sprayed and glittered, splashing off boulders and shining like diamonds as it tumbled to the crystalline pond below. Everything seemed perfect in this

place—the soft meadows, strong trees and above us, the kindly sun on a beautiful spring day. the cliff, the pond, the meadow, the trees, and above us the sun on a beautiful spring day. At first the roar of the crashing water shut out all other sounds, but after a while I could hear a song *within* the roar. The water, like all of Nature, had its own music. The falls cast a cloud of mist, and within it was a rainbow. Again, I had discovered a place that must be like heaven. I cheered loudly, set down my burden, took off my clothes, and jumped into the pond.

Bear did not follow me right away, as the crashing waters were new to him. But after watching me have fun for several minutes, he splashed in to join me.

My favorite thing to do in the great room of our cave was to float on my back and look up at the gold sparkling in the torch light. It was almost like stars. In this majestic outside pond I floated on my back and took notice of the waterfall's surroundings.

I could smell berries, and I knew that is what Bear had smelled to bring us this way. Indeed, there were dense and abundant blackberry brambles on the north shore that grew from the meadow to half-way up the cliff, attended by a multitude of bees and butterflies. I understood why deer were so plentiful there.

In the sunniest corner of the pond, the berries were ripe, and since brambles hung down over the water, Bear was soon swimming underneath, having a feast right there in the water. I joined him, laughing and floating on my back, picking the berries with one hand. It was such a delight!

As I reached the rocky edge of the pond, I felt tree and bramble roots in the water. I could hold to the roots with my left hand and with my right pick and eat berries. When I'd picked the choicest fruits from one branch, I'd feel for the next root and pull myself under the next limb. Having almost had my fill, I reached for the next root, and as I pulled, it wiggled in my hand. Then I felt a sting like fire.

I stood up out of the water and raised my left hand to see a copperhead snake hanging by its fangs. I shook it off and ran to the shore with great dread—*I was snakebit!*

My hand felt like it was burning, and I feared

that I was in grave danger. Father had once been bitten by a copperhead at our sawmill when I was eight. It was a four-foot, fully-grown snake in late summer, and had bitten his calf near his knee. I remembered how he was in great pain and sick for many days. He said his whole body hurt. I had asked him on the second day if he was going to die. "No son," he said, "I will live, but had that snake bitten you, you would surely not survive." It is for that reason I've always believed I would die if a copperhead ever bit me.

I got out of the pond, knelt by my clothes, and tied my shirt sleeve around my left wrist. Bear came out of the water and stood beside me. He recognized I was behaving peculiarly.

"Copperhead got me!" I told him.

After staring at the injury on my left hand, I looked at Bear. There in his mouth was the copperhead snake, which was dying. (Snakes die slowly, even if their heads are removed.) Bear had been right beside me in the water and had seen my misfortune. When I had loosed the snake, he had gone after it.

The snake was small, about two feet, and that

concerned me. Father had explained that young copperheads can't control their venom yet, so every time they bite, they use a full dose of poison. Older snakes sometimes don't use any venom with a bite, or may use a smaller amount. Also, I realized I wasn't a small boy anymore, but a man the size Father was when he was bitten. I assured myself I would live, and I tried to stay calm.

I took out my knife and cut between the fang-marks about a half inch deep. I sucked out blood and spat several times, then rinsed my mouth with water from the pool without swallowing. I then drank a goodly amount of fresh water and washed my hand. I sliced open my food sack to make a bandage for the wound.

"I'm sorry to spoil our holiday like this, Bear," I said. "I wasn't thinking about what I was doing."

Bear had dropped the copperhead on the ground. It had finally stopped writhing. Bear looked at me, wondering if I needed the snake.

I flung the snake into the pond. "It's all right, Bear," I said.

I rolled out the deer hide and sat on it, wondering how much worse the pain would become. My whole arm hurt and twitched, and my insides were in turmoil. Soon I began to vomit. Even when my stomach had been completely emptied, it continued to heave. After I collapsed on the deer hide, the last thing I remembered was that my left hand was red and full.

I woke up in the night. I was very cold, but covered in sweat. All of my limbs were in pain, and I couldn't feel anything in my left arm. With difficulty, I put on my shirt, which had only one sleeve, then collapsed again. As I lay in the grass, I looked at the full moon and whispered, "Thank you, Jesus, that I have not died. Please, help me. Heal me."

Before I fell asleep again, I was overcome with a feeling of peace and comfort. I awoke in the noonday sun with one leg of my pants covering my head. I must have found the pants at sunrise and put them over my face. I sat up and rubbed my face, then realized I was doing so with my left hand. The swelling was almost gone and my hand was no longer red, but just a little red around the cut on my hand.

I washed my bandage in the water to remove

the dried blood. My skin felt hot, so I waded into the water and floated on my back. The water felt very cold, but brought relief. I had sun-burnt myself the day before, and my present discomfort was more from that than snake venom. I felt I might be able to eat food in a short while.

I ventured to the deeper section and let the falling water, which was spraying off boulders forty feet above the pond, crash down upon my head and shoulders. It stung at first, but for reasons I do not understand, it soon felt wonderful. I stood under the falls for several minutes, and it had a mystifying effect. I rather forgot where I was and that I was a young man standing in a pond. I felt as if I were part of the water, part of the stream, and part of the mountain itself. I lost my orientation and fell over in the water.

When I came back up, I saw a herd of deer standing in the meadow, coming toward the pond to drink. I realized this meant Bear was not near. I was sure he was fine, and I lowered myself so as not to startle the deer.

Again, I felt I part of the pond, and held very

still as the deer came to drink. A doe and her fawn drew near, and I watched as they drank their fill, then returned to the wood. Other deer came as well. I do not know how long I watched the deer, feeling completely at ease and part of everything around me, as they came to drink.

Suddenly, all the deer fled into the woods, and I knew Bear was coming back. I came out of the water, and waved, shouting, "Bear!" I heard him bellow happily as he came down the deer path from above the waterfall.

He lumbered into the meadow and rubbed his muzzle on my shoulder.

"I am fine, Bear," I assured him, and rubbed his head and neck.

Bear belched, and by the odor I could tell his stomach was full of berries, roots, grubs and maybe honey. Sure enough, there was a dead bee in his fur behind his left ear.

He began to roll in the grass. I had lain* down, too, and opened my pack to eat some of the nuts. I had thought to do some fishing—the pond had very large fish. It was a great place for fish, as so many brambles were perched at the edge of the pond, and dropped their fruits in the water for fish to eat. Big fish could eat little fish, and what a feast a man could have who fished that pond!

As I ate almonds and pecans, looking up at the waterfall, I thanked Jesus that I was still whole and living, and that I had Bear with me. I had thought to use my fish traps, but my conscience was troubled. Yesterday, I had for a time, expected to die. But I was alive and grateful. I had a feeling that I can only describe as peace and holiness. I closed my eyes and thought of God. With Mother and Father gone, I concluded God was my teacher, and my lessons were books, the Holy Bible, Bear, and Nature. The waterfall was a lesson to be learned, the cave was a lesson, the copperhead was a lesson, meeting the Cherokee men was a lesson, even my own life is a lesson.

I thought about the lessons written in the Holy Bible. God had told to Moses, "Thou shall not kill." I began to think about that. Bear's mother killed my father and my father killed Bear's mother. Father and I killed many animals, fish and turkeys,

Bear just killed a copperhead, and every day birds eat bugs. That is killing.

Everything kills something. Why would God have said that to Moses? God not only said that, he wrote it with his finger when he made it one of the Ten Commandments.

Even God killed, and when Jesus caused the fishermen's nets to fill so much their boats almost sank, Jesus killed fish. I thought there must have been a reason God said that to Moses. God can give and take life, but men ought not to.

Then I remembered what Jesus said:

> All things whatsoever ye would that men
> should do to you, do ye even so to them:
> for this is the law and the prophets.

Mother and Father said that was the "Golden Rule." And Jesus was telling his followers that was what the scriptures meant. That one rule is simpler than Ten Commandments, and it seemed to explain everything very well.

Why do we have to kill each other? I thought. Bear's mother killed my father because she was afraid that we might harm her cub. And Father killed Bear's mother in our defense. I concluded that both were right. It was only common sense.

When I thought about all of the Ten Commandments, they mostly seemed to make common sense. However, I wondered why God had to make a commandment about days—I was only sure of seasons—and bowing down to carved things is simply silly. The only things that have ever made me feel like falling low with awe and wonder have been God's creations—the great room of the cave, a rainbow, and this beautiful waterfall.

I knew my parents were with God, in a place where everything was right. Here on earth, things are not always right. Here we need the Golden Rule, and it came from God. The Holy Bible came from men who talked with God, but Nature is straightway from God without any middling agencies.

When I read a book, it reveals the wisdom of the writer. When I look at the furnishings in my home, they reveal the wisdom of my father, and in places there are unperfected parts where I helped. The Golden Rule is the best wisdom of the Holy Bible, but most of that large book seems to be full of unperfected things men wrote.

What God made directly is Nature, and wisdom and great lessons are everywhere in it. Jesus taught lessons from Nature. I wondered how many of his Nature lessons were never written down for us. There must be many.

I spent the day thinking about Nature, watching the birds, the rabbits, the squirrels, the bugs, the eagles, and the deer. I saw vividly—like never before—that people are animals like any other. We all have eyes, ears, noses, teeth, tongues, feet, and toes. We all protect our babies. We all love, fear, wonder, and have common sense.

And we all want to live. I knew then that I did. So I wondered if I really needed to kill anything. Nature provided all the food I needed and all I had to do was pick it. There were apples, peaches, pears, nuts, roots, edible leaves, and berries aplenty. The squirrels didn't have gardens, I thought, but they ate the same things I ate. I realized that I needn't kill anything. Everything wants to live and raise their babies—all of us.

Even if the birds eat grasshoppers, snakes eat

frogs, and bobcats eat rabbits, it was to mankind that God said "Thou shalt not kill" and gave the Golden Rule. I resolved that I would never again kill any living thing I didn't have to. At that moment, I truly knew what Jesus meant by the Golden Rule.

I built a fire pit in the meadow. I built it high, like the altars in the Holy Bible. I put kindling of needles and twigs upon it, then I took apart my fish traps and placed them on top. I lit the fire and looked up at the red and golden evening sky above the waterfall.

"Thank you, Nature, for your lessons today," I said. "Thy will be done on earth as it is in heaven. I will live by the Golden Rule. I will replant Father's gardens and orchards, and with fruits and nuts I will not ever kill any thing again, unless I absolutely must in defense."

Bear came to my side with a blackberry branch in his mouth, which he dropped beside me. He was still concerned for me. He sniffed my left arm, then licked it several times. It had sunburn and many insect bites, which I would treat with acorn tannin water when we returned home. He cared for me. I was his mother and father, even though I wasn't a bear. We can all be a family. Bear and I are family. I loved Bear and Bear loved me.

"No more fishing for me," I told Bear. "Every thing I need was here well before I needed it. The earth was here, the air was here, the water was here, the sun was here, the trees were here, the fruit and vegetables—every thing I ever needed is here right now, Bear."

In the Holy Bible, Jesus said not to worry about what to eat, drink or wear, because God always provides what we need.

I ate the berries he brought me as the sky turned dark and the stars came out. The moon had not yet shown. I let the fire die, and I lay on my back looking at the heavens. Oh, what a sight to behold! This universe is so beautiful! Surely, I have been so blessed! The moon rose in the sky, shining down its lesser light. I thanked God again, for giving me a taste of heaven on earth. Oh, what peace I truly had!

I fell asleep, but woke when Bear stood up, sniffing the air. "Lie down, Bear."

Bear lay down, but started to growl.

"Quiet, Bear. It's all right."

Bear was quiet. I listened. I heard footsteps.

Creatures were entering the meadow, approaching the pond. I wanted to see if they would pass us by. Then I heard voices—the strange tongue of the Cherokee.

I remained still, Bear also, as two men and a horse approached. In the moonlight at some distance Bear and I must look like a boulder or a mound of earth. We were leeward,* so they could not smell us.

When they were about fifty feet away, I spoke. "I greet you, brothers." I spoke as Nathaniel had greeted me.

The men stopped, and the horse jumped.

The men spoke again in Cherokee, and I didn't understand.

I didn't want to terrify their horse, so I said, "Stay down, Bear. It's all right." Then I spoke again to the men. "I am James, and with me is Scar Nose Bear."

The larger of the two men spoke, still in Cherokee, then began to walk toward me. In his hand he held a knife. I hoped he had friendly intentions. My knife, which I would dread to wield, was in its leather sheath in my pack.

I raised my hand to him and looked to the sky. "Friend," I said. "Friend!"

The man stopped, but still held his knife before him. The second man was on the other side of his horse, and I could tell he was nocking an arrow on a bowstring. I don't know if they were meaning me harm or being cautious, but I felt it was time to properly introduce my companion.

"Up, Bear," I said, asking Bear to perform his favorite trick. "Up!"

Bear rose up onto his hind legs and waved his paws. The two Indians saw a giant, black figure rise beside me, seven feet tall.

"Say hello, Bear," I said. "Speak, Bear."

The men and their horse all leapt back. The bowman dropped his weapon to steady his horse.

"Hhhoooooowwwrrrrrmmmm," spoke Bear.

The men and horse fled back to the treeline, with the horse nearly dragging the smaller man. As they did, I fetched my knife and tied it to my waist. Bear remained standing, and rocked back and forth on his hind legs. He seemed to be laughing in a bear fashion.

"Good boy, Bear," I said. "It's all right. Down, Bear. Lie down."

Bear lay down, and I rubbed his head.

"Friend!" I called again. I looked at Bear and murmured, "Stay, Bear." I walked twenty paces, then picked up the bow and arrow the smaller man had dropped. I held these over my head and walked toward the treeline. "Friend," I called.

The larger man came out from the trees and raised his hand. "Friend," he said. He was my height, bare-chested, and his skin was covered with tattoos. He was an imposing sight. I was also bare-chested and wearing deerskin and a knife. Were it not for my red hair and unmarked skin, I would easily be taken for an Cherokee.

"Do you speak English?" I asked.

"No Eng-hish," he replied, then he pointed into the meadow at Bear and made two sweeps across his nose with his fingers.

"Yes," I nodded. "Scar Nose Bear." I could tell Nathaniel had kept his word and told his surviving people about the special White man in their lands.

The Indian stretched up, like Bear had done,

then laughed, and laughed hard.

I laughed, too, then handed him his companion's misplaced weapons. I realized that although the man had heard the tale of a White man living with a bear, but did not believe it until now.

The second Cherokee came forward without the horse, which must have been tied to a tree. To my surprise it was not a man, but a woman. She seemed very afraid, but held in her hand a rabbit pelt, offering it to me. She was dressed in deerskin pantaloons and boots. Her long hair was gathered on each side by ribbons, and thereby covered her breasts. She wore a necklace of what I think were sea shells. These were probably not Cherokee from these mountains, but perhaps from the East, taking refuge here with other Cherokee.

I accepted the rabbit pelt, and gestured toward the waterfall. I realized this couple needed water for themselves and their horse, and they didn't feel safe to move freely in the daylight. I felt sorrow for their plight.

With a black bear in their path they could not lead their horse to drink. I gestured for them to come, the way I had seen Nathaniel gesture to his companions. I ran ahead into the meadow and pointed to the opposite treeline and told Bear to go.

Bear obeyed and when he was out of sight, the man and woman came forward with their horse. I waved, then walked away to accompany Bear. I felt bad to have frightened them and taken a pelt, but it happened as it had to.

The danger and fear were not caused by me, but by the terror the White Americans had created for the Indians. The Golden Rule had been forsaken, and I was living freely on their lands, where *they* now must hide.

This pelt would remind me to make gifts for my Cherokee neighbors, which I determined to give to Nathaniel. I would leave them at the cabin for him to find. I would make carved walking sticks of hickory and leather pouches from the dead creatures Bear found, and I would give them dried foods from my harvests.

Chapter 14
NEIGHBORS

*W*inter was approaching again. Bear had left me, and I hadn't seen him in a full month. I didn't fear that he had been killed. He was the biggest bear in the area, and the Indians had taken a vow. I had been making gifts for my Cherokee neighbors for many months. I carved many walking sticks from the year-old branches of a hickory tree felled by the great storm. On each one I engraved:

Js Hill to Cherokee | Golden Rule: Mat. 7·12

In each stick I made details and carved the sun, moon, and stars, and in the center of the handle, the likeness of a bear's face with a scarred nose. Each stick would remind its owner of his White friend and their promise to my bear, and also remind any White people, who might wrest the staff and other property from an Indian, to consider the greatest teaching of Christ. No matter what laws any men might make, what I carved on each staff was the highest law.

The most clever gift I had crafted was a vice for shelling nuts. It was a square walnut hinge in two parts with a foot-long handle. With it, even a child could easily break the shell of any almond or walnut. I also built a table and left it in the cabin and placed upon it all my weekly gifts.

On my tenth visit to the cabin, I realized a person had been there. My gifts had been retrieved, but the nut press remained on the table, and around it were shell shards. The fireplace had been used, and I saw something on the hearth that I hadn't seen in a long time—stockings. Next to the hearth was a knee-high, beautifully painted clay jar with a lid. I raised the lid and saw it was full of some sort of flour or meal. In a corner I saw, beneath the shelf where the bottle and letter sat, two large woven baskets with lids. At first I thought to look inside them, but realized it was someone's private belongings, and I had sworn in writing that this was my honored guest. I must not impose on this space, and I would leave future gifts outside the door in good weather.

On my return journey to the cave, I found a large pile of bear droppings. I hoped it was from Bear, but it may also have been another adult bear, and I knew I must be cautious. The wind was behind me, and the squirrels were low in the trees and not announcing predators, so I was certain I was the largest animal in the woods at the time.

I passed through the field of corn that I planted the week after my waterfall visit. It was now higher than my head. Many of the ears had been eaten by birds and deer, but plenty remained for me. I was happy the corn feed so many animals. I was able to fill my pack from just ten of the more than 300 stalks. I would grind the corn into meal, and this winter I would make cornbread like Mother used to make.

Beyond the cornfield, I left the old creek bed and followed the path to my home. On the trail I saw the imprint of a boot. It was smaller than my foot. There were also peg marks from a walking stick. I supposed this was Nathaniel, though I found it odd that his foot would be so small.

Inside the cave I felt alone again. I wished Bear would return. I thought also about the visitor in the cabin and of the Cherokee. I wished I could speak with another human being. Even the refugee Indians in these mountains had wives and companions. All I had was Bear, and he was out on his own and probably finding himself a mate. I guessed my only companion now was Jesus, whom I couldn't see nor hear, but with whom I spoke anyway.

"I know you have been watching me. I'm sure you approve of the staves I carved, telling people about the Golden Rule. Thank you for the Golden Rule. It is most wise. Please, watch over Bear. And please, I would like to see him again. Oh, and if you could help me find a human friend or a wife, I would be greatly obliged. I am not sure how to find friends or wives, or what is the right way to go about it."

When I finished speaking to Jesus, I figured I would read. I looked at my shelf of 27 books. I had read all of them no fewer than eight times. I thought about Blairsville, where Father bought my two most recent books. Blairsville was also a place where there were women who speak English. But what White woman would ever entertain the thought of living in a cave? None of the people in my books lived in caves if they could help it. I did own a cabin, though.

I got it in my head to visit Blairsville. I didn't know how to get there, except that it was west, past a lake, a day's journey, and that a road appears as you approach it. But how would I buy anything? Should I carve goods and trade them? And how would I negotiate with people? Father grew up in a city, with strangers and houses. I'm sure he meant to teach me more about towns and guide me in having inter-actions with merchants and town folk, but he died too soon. Maybe Nathaniel could teach me. He has lived in White settlements as much as his own.

In my writing box I kept a gold nugget that fell on my head during the great storm. It was the size of a strawberry. Should I exchange this nugget for books, the men of Blairsville will suspect I have gold on my land, and an unwanted inquiry will com-mence. The gold around me didn't belong to me— it belonged to the cave—and the cave belonged to the mountain. Though a deed in Blairsville said this part of the mountain belonged to Father, that was just men's scheming. Mountains belong to the earth, and the earth to God. I only considered trading my nugget because the mountain gave this nugget to me on its own.

Maybe I could fashion this into a coin? I could heat the nugget over a hot fire in my pan, then carve 3 or 4 circular impressions in a hickory plank, and in the impressions hammer the gold flat. I could make a few blank coins and tell folk I traded bear and wildcat furs for them, so prospectors wouldn't come looking here.

But that would be a lie. I had never had occasion to lie before, and the thought didn't set well with me. However, it seemed better to lie than to allow men to plunder the mountain. It was the madness of the Whites Nathaniel had mentioned. The Holy Bible calls it being "given to filthy lucre."

As I thought about the cave's gold, I heard the trap door heave open. "Bear?" I asked. A growl came back, and I went to the mouth of the tunnel. In came my dear brother, Bear.

"Bear!" I called with great delight. "I was hoping you were coming back. Are you going to stay for the winter?"

He squeezed his large self through the tunnel and nuzzled my chest with his head. I hugged him and was so glad to feel and smell him again. "Good boy," I said, laughing as tears filled my eyes.

Though Bear only understands a few words, I told him all about the past month, and about my thoughts of making gold coins to take to Blairsville before the coldest weather came. As I repeated my plan aloud, it didn't sound like a good idea.

"Forget all that," I said to Bear. "Let's go into your favorite room." I took a torch with me into the great room, and walked to where the veins of gold were. Bear jumped into the pond to play. As I looked up at the sparkling yellow streaks, I thought about how smoke never fills the great room, even when I have many torches and a fire pit ablaze. "There must be a natural chimney, Bear."

I gathered kindling and wood from the front room and brought them to my fire pit in the great room. When the fire was burning bright and the walls were shining, I watched the smoke curl up the rough rock walls and saw the smoke disappear through a divide about ten feet above me. "Bear, come," I called.

Bear ignored me.

"Come, Bear," I repeated. "Come!"

Bear rose from the water and stood at my side.

"Good boy," I said. "Now look up there." I pointed and bear looked. "That's where I need to go."

I had only done this once or twice before, but I climbed up on bear's back. Thankfully he didn't mind at all. I crouched on his shoulders, then said, "Up, Bear."

Bear stood, then I stood, and with my arms I pushed myself up into the divide, then followed with my feet. I climbed up a body's length and arrived at a deep, stone shelf. It must have been about twenty feet long and ten feet wide. The eroded earth that was once in this place must have created the silt floor in the great room. I could see firelit smoke rising into this "upstairs" room, and I could feel it passing me by on its way elsewhere. I looked through the divide and I saw Bear still looking up at me. He was very amused, and he stood again on his hind legs and growled. From above he appeared small and curious, like when he was a cub.

I crawled around in the dark on the shelf and soon found a light coming into the cavern from above. It wasn't a very large opening—maybe less than a foot wide. I was excited and shouted, "Bear, I found a natural chimney!"

Chapter 15
PRECIOUS

*J*ust then, the light through the natural chimney turned to darkness, and I faintly heard a voice of some kind. Something—or *someone*—had stood over the fissure at the surface of the mountain!

I returned to the divide, dropped down to Bear's side, then ran from the great room to the tunnel, calling, "Stay, Bear!" and out the trap door. I climbed up the rock face of the mountain, above where the great room would be, until I could see where smoke was coming out of a rock.

Over the rock I saw the top of a sapling wave, and knew a person had just brushed past it. Having climbed this mountain for so many years, I was able to swiftly and silently run up the side and past the rock. To my surprise I saw a woman wearing a blue dress, a green shawl around her shoulders, and a bonnet. She carried a walking stick and a satchel. She was making her way toward the clearing on the mountain that Father and I called "the lookout." It was so strange to see a solitary woman out here, and in fine clothing, too! She didn't seem to hear me behind her.

She got to the lookout and sat on a rock, then opened her satchel. I was only twenty paces behind her, watching, wondering why she was here. Her hair was a dark orange, almost brown, very thick, and bound behind her head by a ribbon under her bonnet. She started to sing. It was so lovely to hear a woman sing again! I could not help but draw closer.

I deftly crawled, slow and low like a stalking cat, until I was just ten paces from her, behind the last walnut before the lookout. She had stopped singing. I saw she had laid almonds, shelled, on her apron and was enjoying them. The sunlit rocks were warm, and this was perhaps the only place around where a person could be warm outdoors in such attire. But how did she know of it?

After she finished the almonds, she lay down on the rock. I dared to crawl yet closer, to the back side of the rock she had been sitting on. I crept on toes and fingertips with my body just an inch from the earth. She started to sing again—I didn't know the song at all—but I closed my eyes and savored it like chocolate. Then she suddenly stopped singing.

"I smell you, Father," she said, then giggled.

I held my breath and felt a pang of shame, realizing my encroachment was ill-mannered.

"I smell you!" she repeated with amusement. "You're not twenty feet away, and you're wearing your new bearskin coat!"

I hadn't noticed that I was upwind, nor had I thought that I smelt of Bear, for surely I did. But, I never would expect an English damsel to read scents in the air and distinguish both man and bear! But I, too, smelled bear on the wind, and heard the snapping of underbrush, coming from behind us in the woods. Bear was coming, following me up the mountainside!

"I am not your father," I spoke.

She stood with alarm. "Show yourself!"

After she spoke, I heard Bear coming toward us faster. I knew she heard him, too. Surely Bear smelled a strange human near me, and he might be protective. I warned her, "My bear is coming. Don't be afraid; I will halt him." I stood up, and she was startled that I had been so near—she had been looking for me among the trees.

Bear came upon the treeline and I waved to him. The woman crouched behind the rock.

"Stop, Bear!" I called. "It's all right. Stop, boy."

Bear stopped, but reared high onto his hind legs and uttered a long complaint. He had just come home to me, and here I was running off with some other creature. He didn't like it. I stood firm until Bear sat and settled.

"Your bear?" she asked increduously.

"He's not *my* bear," I said. "He's his own bear. But we are dear friends."

"You are James Hill?"

"Yes," I said, surprised at first that she knew my name, but I figured anyone in these parts would, as the Cherokee and Creek knew me well by now. "And who are you?"

"I am Precious," she answered, looking up at me so I could see the face under the bonnet. She had a striking face, not like any White person I had ever seen, and with many freckles. Her eyes were black, like those of an Indian.

"Pleased to meet you," I said. "Precious is your name?"

"Yes, that is what my mother called me."

I bowed my head. "I beg your forgiveness for stalking you as I had. I have never had a visitor, at least not one who walks on two legs, wears a bonnet and sings."

"This is your home? Here?"

"Yes."

She held up her walking stick. "You made this," she said. "I have been living in your cabin at the invitation you granted my father. I expected to meet you long before today. I have received your generous gifts, I have seen your bear before, but I have never seen you nor your home. He told me you were the strangest White man he ever met, and that a bear obeys your voice."

"You are Nathaniel's daughter?" I asked.

"His name is not Nathaniel," she answered. "He uses many names with White men. He is grateful that you help his people."

"Aren't they your people, too?" I inquired.

Bear growled and scraped earth toward me.

"Bear wants me to return home with him," I explained. "It is getting colder. Would you join us, or are you expecting your father here?"

"I am not expecting my father. He just appears when he wishes, usually at the cabin. Yes, thank you," she said and smiled, "I will join you."

My heart was in flight like a buck. I had never entertained a guest before, and this was a young woman! What would Mother or Father have said? What is fitting for me to do and say? And why do I feel such a strange excitement? I waved at Bear, "Home, Bear! Home!"

Bear preceded us down the path. Mother had taught me etiquette in salutations, dance, removing my hat, eating with a fork, and extending courtesies to guests and ladies. I offered my hand to help Precious down some of the steeper passes and large stones. She seemed plenty agile on her own, and had a walking stick, so I worried my extended hand might imply an insult. But she took my hand every time I offered, and every time smiled broadly. She seemed dressed and groomed for an affair. I, however, was unwashed, in my deerskins, smeared with clay and charcoal from my fires, and smelling of Bear.

As we entered my home, I asked her if she had been in a cave before. She had many times. I showed her the left side of the first room, where I lived. It was warm and lit by the fire, which I refreshed with several new logs. Being a special occasion, I also lit the fat candles and placed them about. I showed her the right side of the room, where Bear usually slept, and I showed her the bed that had been my parents' and the baskets and chests that held their things. Bear followed, often trying to stand between me and Precious.

"Bear, please go lie down," I said.

Bear did not.

"Well, then go swim!" I said, pointing to the great room.

Bear did not.

"Swim?" Precious asked.

"Yes," I said, gathering two torches and more

logs for the fire pit in the great room. "Follow me. We have a much larger room this way." The great room's fire was still healthy, but I built it larger and placed the torches to make the room glow for our guest.

Precious was enchanted. "This is wonderful!" She touched the water with her hand. "It's clear and not very cold. You can swim or bathe anytime you please—even in the winter!"

"Yes," I said pridefully, and without much thought I asked, "Would you please join me swimming?"

Precious smiled and looked down at the ground.

"I am sorry," I said, looking down, too. "I think I spoke improperly."

Bear jumped into the water. He had grown tired of feeling jealous. He was ready to swim and ignore us for a while.

"Don't be sorry, Mr. Hill," she said. "It was only improper for Whites."

Mr. Hill is what people called my father. Nobody had ever called me that before. It felt strange, as if I were trespassing in Father's place. "Please, call me James," I said. "I am eighteen years old. Are we close in age? And do you have a last name?"

"I am nineteen," she said. "My mother's last name was Taylor."

"Your mother is White?"

"Yes, but my mother is dead. She died when I was a child."

I led her back to the front room, and offered her a meal of stewed potatoes, peas, corn, and onions, which she accepted. While the water heated in the pot, I sliced the vegetables and offered her books to read, if she could read. She accepted *A Voyage to New Guinea*, but she continued to tell me the story of her life.

She told me her mother went to school from age ten to fifteen at a church beside a wheelwright, where a fine-looking Indian orphan worked. He impressed her very much, and she felt sorry for how the townsfolk treated him. She fell in love with him, and drew the ire of her family for seeing him again and again. When she became pregnant with Precious, her family disowned her and banished the couple from town, and they went to live amongst the Cherokee. Precious was born, and lived nearly six happy years with her parents until the natives were driven away. The soldiers sent to drive her parents' tribe westward had special orders to take the "half breed" and Nathaniel to the Mississippi and return Precious's mother to her family. She said her mother died not long afterward, maybe from illness, maybe from sorrow, maybe from abuse by soldiers. Precious said she saw her mother's grave stone, which said she died in 1839.

Precious' father never knew his wife had died, and he had sworn to reunite his family. He raised Precious, and worked as a wheelwright and later at a shipyard in New Orleans. He managed to get them both back to the East Coast when she was twelve, only to find his bride's grave. His brother's whole family had died on the forced westward march, and now his wife was dead, too.

Nathaniel felt he had a duty to help oppressed Indians elsewhere, but wanted a better life for his daughter than being a fugitive. He asked his former wheelwright employer to care for Precious and see that she got some education. He thought perhaps if she lived in the same town with her mother's parents, they might embrace her in memory of their daughter. Nathaniel departed, and Precious helped the wheelwright and his wife, who taught her to read, but her grandparents ignored her. When she was fourteen, the wheelwright died, and his frail widow was unable to protect Precious from the townfolk. One day Precious was taken from the street by three men and delivered to Charleston, where she was called a *Quadroon** and made to tend to the needs and whims of sailors.

After a month of this servitude, she managed to steal a dollar from a sailor, flee to a telegraph office, and wire Nathaniel's employer in New Orleans that if he should see or hear from her father, to notify him of her whereabouts and circumstances. Six months later her father appeared in the night and beat her overseer terribly, took the overseer's money, and fled with her on a stolen horse to Springfield, Georgia. He cut her hair and dressed her as a boy, and put her on a train with ten dollars to Gainesville, then wired a White ally there to receive her, and see that she was given shelter among the Creek

Indians hiding in the wilds of North Georgia.

It was a most amazing and awful story. I wept as I heard it. When she had finished the telling, the stew was boiled and ready to serve. But before coming to the table, I felt I should present myself meet* for the occasion, and in accordance with her attire.

"Will you please excuse me?" I asked. "I want to make myself presentable."

"Will I be safe alone with the bear?"

I paused. Bear was sleeping. "You should be," I answered.

Then I went to where Father's things were and retrieved his good shirt. I also took his gray woolen pants. I had never put them on before, but now seemed the right time. I also fetched the hat and coat Father bought me. Then I ran to the great room, flung off my deerskins and plunged into the water. Quickly I scrubbed my whole body with silt and water, then got out and rubbed myself nearly dry by the fire pit, put on the pantaloons, Father's shirt, and my hat and coat, then returned to the table.

Precious laughed when she saw me, but said I looked handsome. I served my guest and seated myself across from her. "Tea!" I exclaimed. "May I serve you tea?"

She laughed again and nodded.

I put on the kettle and gathered dried sumac off the shelf and placed it within. I hadn't made tea since Mother was alive. I had gathered the sumac to try to make candle wax from it.

I was so joyful to have Precious' company that I devoured my soup like Bear, then told her all about my life—my parents' recollections of England, my childhood in the cabin, working with Father in the sawmill, Mother's death, my unpleasant day in civilization, Father's death, how I came to live with Bear, and how I met her father, whom I called Nathaniel. I feared I had exhausted her with my biography and asked if it had been tiresome.

She smiled like an angel, sighed deeply, staring into my eyes, and said, "I would like very much to swim with you, now."

I felt my whole body turn warm. "Would you first like another cup of tea?"

"No, thank you," she said, then rose from her chair and began to walk toward the great room.

I gathered every torch I had and wood for the fire pit and followed her. I ensured the great room was abundantly lit—for safety, of course.

I told her she may disrobe in my absence, and then call from the water once she was in up to her shoulders. It had been since I was seven that I had swum with anyone but Father or Bear. My family used to swim together frequently. When I was about six mother would wear bloomers and a camisole, and then when I was about eight she would stay ashore.

Then I remembered my mother's clothing. "Wait—I have a camisole and bloomers you can wear," I called.

"Do you think that would be more appropriate, James?" Precious asked with a giggle. I wasn't sure why that amused her.

"I don't really know," I replied. "I just want to do the proper thing for you." Then I remembered that Father and I buried Mother in her camisole and bloomers, and I felt ashamed for forgetting.

"James," Precious called from the great room, "the proper thing for you to do is swim."

Swim we did. We splashed, we swam underwater, we laughed. After a while Bear joined us, and he no longer seemed jealous of Precious. I warned her to give him room when he swims—an accidental sweep from his claws could draw blood.

Precious told me that when she was a girl, living with her parents, sometimes half the tribe would swim together—six or seven whole families at once—men and women, children and the aged. She never expected to swim in the month of November, though, much less in a cave.

When Bear got out of the water, Precious and I floated on our backs. I saw her looking at the veins of gold high up in the cavern walls.

"Precious?" I asked.

"Yes, James."

"Do you have the White man's madness?"

"I—I don't think so."

"Have you ever seen gold before?"

"Yes," she answered. "Its in these hills and mountains. White men are mining it wherever its found. That's gold up there if I'm not mistaken."

I was hesitant to affirm. "Yes, and I don't want

White men coming here to take it. Nor do I wish to take it myself."

"Good," she said. "Then you don't have the White Man's madness, either. The Creek people find gold in many places, and they tell nobody. They know it only increases the sorrow and madness of men."

"It's better to leave it where it is," I said, staring up at it. "It looks heavenly ... like heaven, what God's paradise must look like."

"It does," she said. "It feels so peaceful and safe in here with you, James. This place seems magical. This day seems magical—the way you just appeared behind me, with a bear who obeys you, and then treated me with so much kindness, prepared me a meal, and now we're swimming inside a mountain under a canopy of sparkling gold! I fear this is a dream and it will all vanish when I wake up."

"Are you a Christian?" I asked.

"I might be," she said. "I'm not sure. My mother told me stories from the Bible when I was small, and some of my father's tribe were Christians. Even my father knew about Jesus and spoke well of him, but he believes the White man is ill-suited for Christianity. He feels they can not comprehend the teachings of Jesus well enough to practice them."

"I practice them," I said. "That is why I put the Golden Rule on everything I make." I recited the Golden Rule to her, and she said the Cherokee had the exact same teaching. I was so glad to hear that, and I had suspected they must. She also told me that the wheelwright and his wife taught her to read from the New Testament, and they took her to church several times.

I asked her if she was baptized. She said she hadn't been—nobody among the Whites asked her or offered the rite to her.

"Well, that's all that's left to do!" I said.

"How is it done?"

"In the New Testament the baptized believers would baptize other believers. That's all." For the first time I realized I had no idea why being dipped in water was part of Jesus's teachings, and why churches continued to do it. White men disregarded the Golden Rule when it came to all other races, and even certain kinds of other White people, and churches were clearly not correcting such abominations while continuing to baptize.

Obeying the Golden Rule seemed of incalculably higher value than getting dipped in water. But I guessed baptism was an act of faith Jesus requested. It made little sense, but we should do it because he asked. It seemed very fair, actually, because *anyone* could be baptized. Had Jesus asked something spectacular, like "tame a bear," I would find myself all alone up in heaven with handful of carnival workers.

Precious stood directly in front of me in the water and asked, "Would you baptize me, then, James?"

"Yes, certainly!" And then I remembered our complete nakedness, which I'd only forgot but that past minute. "But, I would … have to touch you," I said. I felt my whole body turn warm again.

"Isn't baptism of greater importance than a moment's immodesty?" she asked.

"That is a very wise summation," I said, then realized I wasn't exactly sure how baptism was done, either. But if baptizing was something one person did to the other, and the person being baptized was covered, then uncovered in the water, it couldn't be too elaborate. I remembered a verse about baptism:

> Therefore we are buried with him by
> baptism into death: that like as Christ
> was raised up from the dead by the glo-
> ry of the Father, even so we also should
> walk in newness of life.

"So," I said with a trembling heart, but confi-
dent voice, "baptism is a burial and resurrection in
the water. So lie in my arms, and I will put you under the water, then bring you back up."

She smiled so beautifully that some calm returned to me. She placed her right leg over my right
forearm and her back into my left, then brought her
left leg up so that she was lying in my arms. I wish I
could say I executed this rite without a single glance
at her body, but I did behold her form a great deal.
I could scarcely breathe for the sight—much different than a man. In my whole collection of books
were three likenesses of nude women by artists'
hands—Eve, a statue of Venus, and Queen Cleopa-
tra. Again, I say that seeing a drawing is not at all
the experience of seeing a living thing.

I felt I should say something, but in the whole

New Testament I don't remember anything being recited before a baptism, so I just said, "Precious, now receive your baptism," then bent my knees to go under the water with her, but when I descended down she floated on the surface. I feared I had given myself her baptism! Of course, since I was baptized in my infancy, and God knows all things, I was sure the Lord would still count us both adequately baptized at the end of the day. I had to rise back up and rethink my method. "I am sorry," I said in a whisper. "I will have to press you down, then pull you up."

"Please do," she whispered back.

Though it was she going under the water, I held my breath, then placed my left palm high on her chest and my right palm low on her abdomen and submerged her. Down she went. I reached beneath her and pulled her back.

"Thank you," she said, holding to my arms.

I looked to see if her appearance had changed. I was uncertain what to expect, this being the first baptism I'd ever witnessed. As I stared at her, I did believe she was aglow in some way. I felt all aglow, too, and like never before in my life.

"Are you well, James?" she asked.

I was breathing heavily, and maybe I was shaking a little. "I just … I just am so happy for you," I said. But I knew that wasn't all, and I felt like I would be lying if I didn't say more. "And I am just so happy you are here."

Her smile grew even larger and her face shone like fine gold.

"It is like heaven sent you," I said. "I wish you had no cause to ever leave."

"Do you want me to stay?" Precious asked.

"Would you if you could?"

"I can, and yes, I would," she said. "I am alone in the cabin, visited only twice in many weeks, once by my father, and once by a Creek messenger."

"Why don't you live among the Creek or the Cherokee?" I asked.

"Because they are going to move again, the last Creek families will go to Alabama, and the Cherokee to North Carolina. My father wanted me in your cabin so that if a militia comes they might leave me in peace for your sake. He fears for me marching to another state, like he did years ago, when all his relatives died. Because I am part White, and have lived half my life among Whites, he would have me live a better life with them, and to find a husband among them."

"Stay with me, then," I begged.

"I will stay," she said.

We were so overjoyed with our decision that we embraced, but released in the name of propriety. Still, nothing about the whole day seemed shameful. In truth, the memory of that day now seems as beautiful and holy as my sabbath at the waterfall.

Precious and I came out of the water like Adam and Eve. Most of the torches had gone out and the fire was low. I blew on the coals and arranged the remnants of the sticks and logs so the fire would increase. We stood by the fire to dry, speaking not a word, but smiling much and exchanging many glances. She had bloomers and put only them and her blouse on. I put on Father's woolen pants and his linen shirt.

We returned to the table and talked more about our plans. It became dark and cold, and no time to be traveling, so we determined she would stay the night, and on the morrow I would go with her to retrieve her things, which together we could move in a single trip.

I would leave a letter for Nathaniel to stay at the cabin, should he visit, and I would visit every other day to look for him. I, of course, would ask his blessing for his daughter remaining in the cave with me, and show him the whereabouts of its entrance.

I considered how we should sleep. My bed was just large enough for myself, and no one had lain on my parents' large bed since Father died. I would check it for spiders and take its fur covering outside for dusting. "I'll prepare the large bed for you," I said.

"And you," she replied.

"No, I'll sleep here in my bed."

"James, if I am to live here with you, in your care and protection, wouldn't you desire to have in return my warmth and the comfort of my close companionship? And do you wish for my father to consider you as the answer to his prayer that I find a husband among the Whites? Or are you considering me as only a temporary guest?"

Again she had issued a most wise summation, and it took my breath away. "You make the most keen observations," I said. "By all means, we will both sleep in the large bed!"

Together we shook out the fur covering outside, Bear came out with us and manured his customary thicket, and I showed her where the latrine areas were. Inside, we together moved the large bed closer to the fireplace. She suggested a reordering of the furnishings in the front room, and again her logic was profound. As I helped her reorganize the cave, I felt such an excitement to be sharing my space and time with another person again, and such a beautiful and agreeable one.

Finally, we both lay under the covering. With the fire it was too warm, and Precious removed her clothing. I was unsure whether to remain in mine, but I thought of Adam and Eve in the garden, naked and unashamed, then removed mine as well. When the fire died and the room cooled, Precious pressed herself close to me. She put her head on my chest, and I listened to her breathe. I could not sleep. Soon she had an arm across me, then also her leg. My heart was pounding, and I knew that even Bear's snoring couldn't prevent her from feeling or hearing it. Then she rose up over me and put her mouth to mine and kissed me—Oh! how I had wished for that! We kissed more, and slowly, and inhaled each others' breath. We embraced each other as fully as any man and wife could, and our union was holy.

That night, I learned what it is to have a wife, and the bond that causes a man to cleave to his woman. I had prayed for a companion, and that very day I had been given one. We did not manage to go to the cabin to get her things the next morning; rather we remained in the cave, talking, swimming, returning to the bed, and almost forgetting to eat. The next two days were bitterly cold outside, so we continued much the same. I gave to her all of my mother's things, so she now had a coat made by my father, deerskin boots, and a ring for her finger. On the fifth day we went to the cabin, left the letter for Nathaniel, and brought back her things.

When we returned to the cave, Bear was gone. A week passed and he still hadn't returned. Precious and I had made our union so evident, rearranged the home, and I had paid him so little attention, that it didn't surprise me that he took leave of us.

Bear didn't return for the whole winter. I spent all my time with Precious, teaching her things I'd learnt from Father and Mother, and she taught me what she knew of Indian ways and the Cherokee language.

Nathaniel returned mid-winter, and was glad to discover I had taken his daughter to wife. He promised to return again in the spring with a few people of the Cherokee tribe for a Cherokee-style wedding. He described how his people […]

At this point one or two pages appear to have been missing, and the final page was partially stained and torn, and went as follows.

[…] sure Nathaniel would survive. The soldiers left the mountain after two weeks. The dogs would have found the cave were it not for Bear's return, and I am glad the soldiers did not shoot him, too. I managed to wash the blood from the blue wedding blanket and told Nathaniel he could remain with us for as long as he needed.

One month later our baby was born. Oh! what a time! I feared for Precious, but Nathaniel knew what to do, and Precious birthed our son in the cave pond. I looked upon the face of the child God gave us and my life began anew. I promised Precious, the baby, Nathaniel and God that I would be the father to him that my father was to me. I cut the cord and treated her with herbs.

I named my son after his mother's father and after my father's father—Nathaniel Augustus Hill. Nathaniel gave him a Cherokee name, Unega Awohali, which means White Eagle. I would now call my father-in-law only by his Cherokee name, Agowati[tha] […] two more weeks, then would move to the cave where the Cr[eek India]ns previously hid la[… *missing*] for food for the coming winter.

Our lot could perhaps be remedied [if we mined] some of the gold, but it [was our sacred] vow never to do so. The go[ld that the mountai]n gave me could purchase fo[r us …] and some official in Union County pers[uade …] for my family and […], which should be our lawful […].

EPILOGUE

SUCH IS HOW THE LAST PAGE ENDED. I don't know if James Hill lost the diary, nor do I know what happened to him, his wife, their baby, or the gold. I never looked for the cave because I am too old. Maybe it is there, maybe it was mined long ago, I don't know.

What impressed me most from this story was here was a young boy who lived entirely off the land and who grew up with no money, no society, no church, no guns, no formal education, and no government, but with happiness in doing whatever he found along his journey through life. When I think about his life and all that he experienced and how he handled situations, I see just how simple life can be. *Not easy—just simple.*

If the James Hill story is true, and if there is gold here in this area, I hope it is not found, because as James Hill believed, the lovers of gold would destroy heaven on earth.

Appendix A
GLOSSARY OF ANTIQUATED AND OBSCURE TERMS

an hundred – *adjective* – one hundred (British).

amongst – *preposition* – among (British).

artifice – *noun* – the work of creating an artifact.

bade – *verb* – past tense of **bid**, meaning to express a preference or request.

corduroy – *noun or adjective* – a road or path constructed of cords, being logs of fixed length, usually split with flat surfaces facing up, arranged perpendicular to the direction of the road, generally topped with sand. Corduroy roads first appeared in Roman times and continued to be constructed and used into the 20th Century. It is from corduroy roads that corduroy fabric got its name.

countenance – *noun* – appearance, behavior; later came to reference primarily facial expressions; *verb* – to look upon with approval.

craft – *noun* – skill or an occupation requiring skill.

cunning – *adjective or adverb* – skillful, resourceful.

fast – *adverb* – tightly; the origin of fasten; *examples:* shut fast, hold fast, and the modern term colorfast (color-retaining).

fetter – *noun or verb* – shackle; from the archaic verb **fet**, meaning to bind or secure.

fine beans – *noun* – British term for green beans.

gilded – *adjective* – covered in gold; sometimes rendered **gilt**.

haberdasher – *noun* – a merchant who sells clothing accessories and sometimes clothing.

haberdashery – *noun* – the haberdasher's store, more likely to offer accessories (buttons, thread, needles, hats, belts, scarves, kerchiefs) than the wares or services of a clothier, tailor, or seller of whole cloth (fabrics).

hail – *verb* – greet, salute, draw attention.

hasten – *verb* – past tense of **haste**, meaning to hurry.

hempen – *adjective* – made of hemp fibers.

hewn – *adjective* – cut, from the past tense of the verb **hew**, meaning to cut.

ides – *noun* – the midpoint of a month.

keen, keenly – *adjective, adverb* – proficient, accurate, superior, well developed.

lain – *adjective* – the state of having been laid down, formerly used as the past perfect tense of **lie**.

leaf – *noun* – a single sheet of paper.

leathern – *adjective* – made of or pertaining to leather.

leeward – *adjective, adverb* – ahead of the course of the wind. A leeward creature may detect the scent of something windward.

manifold – *adjective* – various, multiple, multi-part, many times; *examples:* manifold ways, manifold rewards.

meet – *adjective* – suitable; *example from GENESIS 2:20 (KJV):* "but for Adam there was not found an help[er] meet for him."

multitude – *noun* – a group of many things or persons.

natural history – *noun* – the study of biology or other natural sciences.

nock – *verb* – to position an arrow on a bowstring in preparation for drawing and shooting.

quadroon – *noun* – a person who is thought to be one quarter African and three quarters Caucasian (one minority grandparent). An **octoroon** was a person one-eighth African (one minority great-grandparent).

righting and wroughting – *phrase* – American colonists placed great value on ingenuity and craftsmanship, as the economy depended greatly on building infrastructure (homes, roads, canals, bridges) and manufactured or refined goods for sale and export. Though American heroes like Washington and Jefferson had classical educations, the popular sentiment, which was often expressed, was that righting (repairing) and wroughting (construction) were more practical and profitable skill sets.

sawn – *adjective* – having been sawed.

slinger – *noun* – one who hunts or fights in battle using a sling as a weapon.

smite – *verb* – to strike or impact.

smithy – *noun* – the workshop of a smith, being a tradesman who fabricates goods from raw materials, such as metal, stone or wood.

smote – *verb* – past tense of **smite**.

spangled – *adjective* – dotted, spotted, flecked; derived from the verb **spangle**.

spilt – *adjective* – the state of being spilled; *verb* – past tense of spill. The use of -*t* in place of -*ed* was common from medieval times, but some past tense verbs are still commonly rendered this way, such as dreamt, spent, and swept.

storey – *noun* – British for **story**, a level of a building, pluralized with -*s*, rather than -*ies*.

sundry – *adjective* – various; *example:* "at sundry times and in sundry places."

thoroughfare – *noun* – a main road or street, one which leads to or through other roads.

tinderbox – *noun* – a device that used flint and steel for igniting; the precursor to modern cigarette and barbecue lighters.

vast – *adjective* – expansive, extensive, broad, enormous, far-reaching.

warren – *noun* – a rabbit's home.

Appendix B

FURTHER STUDY

LIKE JAMES HILL IN THIS BOOK, we should all consider ourselves students, even if going through a subject alone. This book is easy to read and can be understood on its own, but it is rich with many historical, natural, cultural, and literary references. To get the most out of a book such as this, a better understanding of these subjects makes the story come alive, and may even help the reader extract teachable life lessons.

Below are several categories of fields of study relative to *A Mountain of Gold* that educators and self-educators may wish to research and discuss. Subjects that are pervasive in the book are marked with an asterisk (*).

GEOGRAPHY

Cherokee Nation (19th Century)*
Brasstown Bald Mountain, Georgia
Union County, Georgia

Blairsville, Georgia

Port of Charleston, South Carolina

CULTURE

The Five Civilized Tribes

Cherokee wedding ceremonies

Quadroon and Octaroon

Women's / Men's attire of 19th Century America

Subterranean dwellings / Cave homes*

NATURE & BIOLOGY

Ore genesis: gold*

Yellow fever

Sumac

Lake trout (fish)

Copperhead (snake)

Peaches

Hickory

American black bear*

Solutional cave*

Shiner (fish)

Blackberry (bush, fruit)

Walnuts

Almonds

Acorns

LANGUAGE & LITERATURE

Authorized (King James) Version*

Noah Webster's *English Dictionary of the American Language*

Thomas Paine's *Rights of Man*

Virginia Declaration of Rights

Captain Thomas Forrest's *A Voyage to New Guinea …*

Lysander Spooner's *Address of the Free Constitutionalists to the People of the United States*

James Gray Smith's *A Brief Historical, Statistical and Descriptive Review of East Tennessee, United States of America …*

Von Humboldt's *Cosmos: A Survey of the General History of the Universe*

Governor William Bradford

Edward Taylor

Cotton Mather

Charles Brockden Brown

HISTORIC EVENTS

The Georgia Land Lotteries*

The Trail of Tears*

Georgia Gold Rush

The Indian Removal Act

1842 Slave Revolt in the Cherokee Nation

Cherokee Nation v. Georgia (1832)

HISTORIC PERSONS

George Wythe

James Madison

Henry Clay

Chief John Ross

Benjamin Franklin

Aelius Galenus

Alexander von Humboldt

Thomas Jefferson

George Mason

Captain Thomas Forrest

John Ridge (Cherokee)

Hippocrates

al-Razi (Razes)

TECHNOLOGY

Tinderbox*

Corduroy roads

Laudanum

Cotton gin

History of book binding

Quinine

Waterwheels

Fur trapping

Blacksmithing

Charred barrel Bourbon

Telegraph (before 1860)

Bowie knife

Wheelwright

Sling (weapon)

PHILOSOPHY

The Golden Rule*

Altruism

Deism

Pantheism

Vegetarianism

Asceticism*

Ahimsa

Original Sin / Redemption

Animism

Anarchy

Other fine books by
Campian Bellstone Publishers

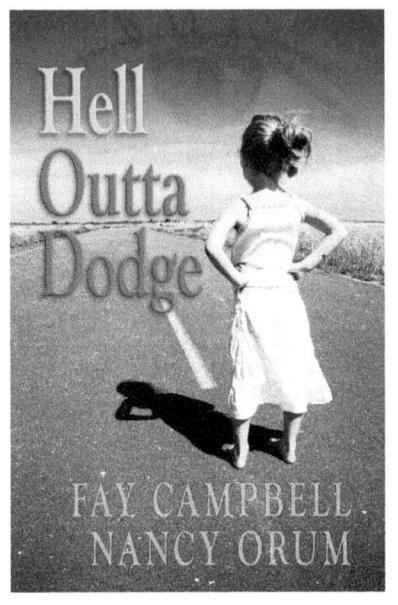

Hell Outta Dodge
is a novel that follows three childhood friends on a long-overdue reunion, coming to terms with conflict, with family, and with the harrowing disappearance of a former classmate. This adventure delivers moving drama, laughter, and hair-raising suspense.

Naked Me
is an assortment of moving poems, lyrics, and short stories about human growth and longing. It contains 43 offerings, many of which beg to be sung. This small book is a tour-de-force of joy, awe, humor, tragedy, and passion.

www.BellstoneBooks.com

www.ingramcontent.com/pod-product-compliance
Lightning Source LLC
Chambersburg PA
CBHW060740180626
46819CB00001B/46